TEEN SPIRIT

Also by Francesca Lia Block:

Weetzie Bat

Missing Angel Juan

Girl Goddess #9: Nine Stories

The Hanged Man

Dangerous Angels: The Weetzie Bat Books

I Was a Teenage Fairy

Violet & Claire

Guarding the Moon

Wasteland

Goat Girls: Two Weetzie Bat Books

Beautiful Boys: Two Weetzie Bat Books

Necklace of Kisses

Blood Roses

How to (Un)cage a Girl

The Waters & the Wild

Pretty Dead

The Frenzy

House of Dolls

Roses and Bones: Myths, Tales, and Secrets

Pink Smog

The Elementals

Love in the Time of Global Warming

FRANCESCA LIA BLOCK

TEEN SPIRIT

HARPER TEEN
An Imprint of HarperCollinsPublishers

HarperTeen is an imprint of HarperCollins Publishers.

Teen Spirit
For information address HarperCollins Children's Books,
a division of HarperCollins Publishers,
10 East 53rd Street, New York, NY 10022.
www.epicreads.com

Library of Congress Cataloging-in-Publication Data
Block, Francesca Lia.
    Teen spirit / Francesca Lia Block. — First edition.
        pages   cm
    Summary: "Julie wanted nothing more than to feel connected
to her deceased grandmother, but when she actually makes contact
with the other side it's not her grandmother that responds, but a
spirit that has its own sinister agenda"—Provided by publisher.
    ISBN 978-0-06-200809-1 (hardcover bdg.)
    [1. Supernatural—Fiction. 2. Spirits—Fiction. 3. Grand-
mothers—Fiction. 4.   Dead—Fiction. 5.   Single-parent
families—Fiction. 6. Dating (Social customs)—Fiction. 7. Beverly Hills (Calif.)—Fiction.]   I. Title.
PZ7.B61945Tee   2014   2013008057
[Fic]—dc23   CIP

Typography by Alicia Mikles
13 14 15 16 17   LP/RRDH   10 9 8 7 6 5 4 3 2 1
❖

First Edition

Thanks to Tara Weikum,
Debbie Edwards, Laurie Liss,
Brandie Coonis, Eve Coquillard,
Nancy Cole Silverman,
Robin Carr, Adam Greenberg,
Jeni McKenna, Emily Dickinson,
Gilda Block (in memory, always),
Jasmine, and Sam.

PROLOGUE

Until things started to fall apart, I had never questioned my desire to be alive. It wasn't something I had to think about. Even though I didn't have any close relationships at school and felt different from the other kids, even though I wasn't always confident about how I looked or the things I could do, I never thought there was something really wrong with me; I was never very lonely or sad. I came from a line of strong women who were my best friends. My grandmother, Miriam, my mother, Rachel, and the house we lived in together: that was all I needed.

My mom bought the house in the Hollywood Hills with money from her writing job at the studios. It was built in the 1940s, Spanish style with a red tile roof, high ceilings, and bleached wood floors. She told me that when she walked down the drive lined with cypress trees, through the arched wooden door, into the empty rooms, she found there were tears on her cheeks and she knew that this was the house where she wanted to live until she died.

I felt the same way. My room was upstairs and overlooked the fig, lemon, and avocado trees that surrounded the pool tiled with *La Sirena*, Mexican mermaids. Banana trees, miniature palms, and birds-of-paradise crowded around like gossiping, lunching ladies, happy to grow there. Grapevines and honeysuckle and jasmine intertwined, draping over a small lattice arbor. When I came home to this house, even at the age of seventeen, I felt the way I did when I was a kid, sweaty and tired and hungry, excited to get a glass of milk and a cookie that my grandmother had baked, lie on the faded Moroccan rug with a book, and read aloud to her, as we waited for my mom to come home. I brought all my problems and worries to my grandma first, and then to my mom, and they were always able to take them away. Somehow I believed that the house helped as well, but it was really my grandmother who healed me the most.

When I was in fifth grade, I told her the names of

the kids in my class, in order of popularity. I had made a careful list in which I was second from the bottom before Jerry Vetch, who was really smart, almost six feet tall, and hummed to himself all day. I did just as well in writing and spelling as he did, although not quite as well in math, and I was too quiet and shy to have any friends.

My grandma asked me, "What makes someone popular, my love?"

"They're better looking."

"Better looking, how?"

"They look like everyone else except better."

"*Bubela*," she said, "you're a beauty. But you don't look like everyone else." She was referring to my nose, which is broader, my lips and hips, which are fuller, and my eyebrows, which are bushier, or used to be before I started plucking them.

"Then I can't be popular," I said. "Or beautiful."

She looked deep into my eyes and asked me, "Are they nicer than other people?"

"No. They're usually meaner to everyone except the other popular kids, except for Ally Kellogg." She was popular, thin, and blond with a tiny nose and butt, and she had signed my yearbook *Have a great summer, Luv always, Ally.* But she was the exception.

"So why would you want to be popular?" my

grandmother asked me. "You're beautiful and nice. Are they smarter?"

"No," I said. "Popular people try not to seem too smart."

"So popular means you look pretty much like everyone else, you aren't too smart, or pretend you aren't, and you're only nice to other popular people?"

I nodded. "And you don't have the dreams."

When I was really little, I started having dreams that scared me so much I'd wet the bed. I sometimes still had them, even in fifth grade. My mom had taken me to a therapist but I didn't like him—he never smiled, my mom called him "dour"—and the dreams only got worse, so I stopped going. My grandmother was the person I would go to when the dreams woke me. She didn't always tell my mom. It was my grandma who changed the sheets and let me climb into bed with her. Sometimes I walked in my sleep, too. More than once she'd found me standing in her doorway and she'd lead me back to my room. I never remembered doing it nor did I remember the dreams, except as little flashes of fear. Eventually my grandmother bought me a Native American dream catcher and hung it above my bed. It was supposed to catch the nightmares in its web and slide the good dreams down its feathers to reach me. Since then the nightmares were more infrequent, but I still had them sometimes.

"You're very special, Julie," my grandmother told me. "Don't forget that. You have gifts." I didn't see how nightmares were gifts, but when she kissed me, I smelled the sweet and slightly bracing fragrance of lavender, and I was comforted. She wore the oil on her skin, put silk bags of the dried flowers everywhere around our house, bought air sprays and soaps with pictures of lavender plants embossed on them.

"I'd rather be like Ally Kellogg," I said.

"Oh, the world never changes, does it? You have to start appreciating yourself for who you are. Promise me that, star shine."

My grandmother reached into her dresser drawer and took out a large photo album covered in red velvet that had faded to pink and was worn away in patches; the carved gold wood medallions on the front were chipped. When she opened the album, I saw that the spine had pulled away and was still attached only by threads. Inside, cardboard frames held browning, faded photographs of men with long beards and women with severely combed-back hair—small sprigs of curls sprouting at the tops of their foreheads—wearing high-collared, wasp-waisted dresses. Some sat in parlors on chairs with claw feet beside potted ferns, and others on wicker benches under misty garden bowers. There was a small, stern-faced girl in black holding a blond doll in white lace that was as big as she was and, weirdly, more alive looking. A young man with a broad face, flared nostrils, a perfect curlicue mustache, and a silk ascot. He looked like he could have been a Russian ballet dancer. Wedding pictures of stout grooms gripping fading, lace brides.

And there was one picture of a young woman, wearing a fur stole with the fox head still attached, sitting at a table with a candelabra, leaning on her elbow. She had my broad nose, full lips, and bushy eyebrows. And, in her own way, I recognized that she was beautiful.

"You see?" my grandmother said.

She went to her closet and came back with a beaded lace dress, which she told me to put on. I spun in front of the mirror, the blush-colored lace making my skin glow. The dress was a little big, but it gave me my first glimpse of myself as a woman.

"Look in the bodice lining," Grandma said.

She had placed a tiny note there. *Your body is electric,* was what it said.

Later that day, Grandma Miriam had me read Walt Whitman aloud to her. "I Sing the Body Electric."

Over time, after spending so many hours with

Grandma Miriam, after ingesting the words of poetry, after working the magical talisman gifts of her vintage clothing and jewelry and shoes and gloves and purses into my wardrobe, I began to feel better about myself, even though I never became popular and I still didn't have any real friends to hang out with except her and my mom. I knew I was okay then. But what I didn't yet realize was that my well-being depended on one strong spirit in a fragile, much too temporal body.

PART I

A Visitor in Marl

MIRIAM

1

Six years after the conversation about popularity, everything in my life changed. It took just one afternoon.

"I love your outfit!" my grandmother said, kissing me when I came into her room. I was wearing the strands of pearls, pointed satin pumps, and pink-and-black tweed jacket she had given me, along with a pencil skirt, a men's white T-shirt, slouchy socks, and my black-framed geek-chic glasses.

"Thanks, Grandma. I wore it for you. And thanks for the note." I took out the tiny peach-colored envelope, embossed with my grandmother's initials and a wreath of flowers, that she had placed in the pocket of the jacket. It said, *You are a thing of beauty in this, my love.*

"The pearls were from your grandpa Maury!" she said, touching them where they lay, warm on my collarbone.

"They are just costume but a nice quality, on sale at Loehmann's. Oh, those shoes hurt my feet!"

"Speaking of which, can I give you a pedicure?" I held up the Seashell nail polish I had bought with her in mind. My mother was going into the office, and my grandma and I had the whole day to do whatever we wanted.

"First, let's eat! Chocolate chip *rugelach*?" It was her family recipe and our favorite thing to have when my mom wasn't there to tell us it wasn't a healthy breakfast choice.

While the pastries baked, glazing the air with the scent of butter and sugar, I took off my grandmother's slippers and tucked a piece of toilet paper between her toes. I painted on the thin sheen of polish, careful not to tickle her.

We ate the crescent-shaped pastries, the chocolate still melting inside, though my grandmother mostly only nibbled hers. Then we cleaned up and I modeled some other outfits for her. She had stories about all of her old clothes. I never got tired of hearing them, but that day she seemed quieter and stopped midsentence a couple of times, forgetting what she had just said.

"I'm fine, sweetie," she told me when I asked if she was okay. "But will you read to me now, Julie? Emily, please. 'A Visitor in Marl.'"

So I sat at her feet and read a particular Emily Dickinson poem she wanted to hear. The book was heavy and gray with yellowing pages and that comforting old-book smell. When she was in college at NYU, my grandmother had faintly underlined some of the titles in pencil, including this one.

"What does 'marl' mean anyway?" I said. I usually loved Emily Dickinson, but that day the poem gave me a graveyard chill that made me pull my sweater sleeves down over my hands and I wanted to stop reading.

"It's a kind of stone. Marlstone. A visitor in stone."

My grandmother sat in her rose velvet armchair, lace doilies on the arms, with her feet propped on the stool. She was dressed in a gauze tunic and pants and Native American turquoise, her white hair piled in a bun, with loose strands falling down around the shell-like bones of her face. I hadn't realized how thin her face was and I wondered if she'd lost weight. She frowned and began to rub her arm.

"Are you okay?" I asked.

"There's something I must tell you, darling," she said.

Her eyes were staring right at me, big and bright green, full of wonder like a child's. She put her hand to her mouth.

"What's wrong?" I could feel a small siren flashing in my chest. "Grandma!"

On that late-summer afternoon, with the sun still shining soft and dustily through the tall arched windows, she put her hand to her heart. And before there was anything I could do, my grandmother slumped in her chair. I took her in my arms and lay her down and opened her mouth and, gently as I could, held her nose closed so I could breathe air into her.

There was already a darkness pooling around her eyebrows, under her skin. She was cold. But when I leaned back to call 911, I noticed that a pale lavender radiance hovered over her body like light through an amethyst, and I could hear music playing, something soft and baroque and strange, otherworldly.

I called 911 and then I called my mom. I don't remember what I said. I held my grandma in my arms, and I watched the lavender light. I could smell the dry powdery sweetness of a lavender plant when you crush the leaves between your fingers, and I could hear the last faint strains of the music, but by the time the ambulance came, my grandmother's body was stiff like a doll's, her eyes now blank, lightless, and empty, and the scent and the sound and the shine around her were all gone.

I didn't tell my mom about the color I saw or the sounds I heard. I figured that the last thing she needed after losing her own mother was to have to take me to the doctor and worry about a diagnosis of some weird neurological condition that was probably only a temporary reaction to grief anyway.

I didn't even tell my mother about the words my grandmother had said, but I thought about them a lot. *There's something I must tell you, darling.* Did she know she was about to die? Was there something important she needed to let me know?

MY MOM AND I held hands as she rang the buzzer in front of a small brick building on the far east end of Melrose. A very tall young man in a loose-fitting black suit let us into a waiting room. He was handsome except for his pasty complexion and teeth that were discolored and protruding. After he offered us coffee, which we declined, he had my mom fill out a form and then went upstairs. I wondered what it was like up there, then tried not to imagine it. Even the downstairs room smelled like death—the burn of formaldehyde and the sick sweet of rot—no one had even bothered to cover up the odor, although they had taken the time to put fake, red plastic roses in a vase and hang framed acrylic seascapes on the walls as if this was just any tacky office. Maybe they didn't smell anything anymore. I remembered the delicate, comforting fragrance that accompanied my grandmother's departure; it filled me with despair to think of it now.

When the man handed my mother the green jade urn with carvings of cranes and peonies, he said, "I'm sorry for your loss," as if he had said it a thousand times.

But no one else had lost *her.*

How could a person you loved be reduced to this? I wondered, looking at the urn. How did a person you loved come to be out of nothing? I thought of my grandmother's baby picture that my mom kept by her bedside. That little girl with eyes the color of the urn I held, and pale hair, the smile like a candle flame. Where did she come from? Where did she go? How was it that I couldn't still touch her or hear her voice, when I had been able to do these things my whole life?

We kept my grandmother's ashes in the urn on the mantelpiece. She had purchased the urn in Chinatown years ago and liked to put fresh pink peonies in it in the spring. My mother and I planned to scatter the ashes in the sea, the way Grandma and my twelve-year-old mother had done with my grandfather Maury's ashes, but I guess neither my mother nor I wanted to make my grandmother's death that real, touching her remains with our hands. So we left her there in the urn. And we left her room exactly as it was, unable to go through her things just yet.

But then everything changed so quickly, as if without my grandmother a spell of protection had been broken, the spell of my never really feeling lonely, even without friends, the spell of my independent mother, the spell of our lovely house where we were planning, in many, many years, with the old trees as witnesses, to peacefully die ourselves.

It began a week after my grandmother's death. Mom came home from her office on the Paramount lot looking a mess, mascara stains on her face and white blouse. And I noticed a gray color around her, a dull haze. I wanted to tell her, but what could I say? *You look gray, Mom?*

I still hadn't even been able to tell her about the lavender light surrounding Grandma Miriam. Was this the same kind of thing? What was wrong with me?

We had plans to order takeout and watch a movie (our comfort drugs of choice), but she'd brought a bag of groceries instead. She took out cold cuts and a loaf of bread.

"What's wrong?" I asked. "I thought it was Pad Thai slash Cocteau night." Then we were going to do our nails Bitter Blue and deconstruct the movie and a pint of Ben & Jerry's simultaneously.

She plopped down at the kitchen table in our sky-and-sunflower-tiled kitchen and stared at the food. I could see a little pinkish liquid around the meat inside the clear plastic packet.

"I lost my job."

"What?"

"I got fired. They're not bringing the show back." She fanned her face and bit her lip as if to keep from crying, but it didn't work. My mom wrote for a supernatural TV drama called *Ghost in the Machine*. Or, used to write for it. The ratings weren't great, but I didn't know it was in danger of being cancelled.

I put my arms around her thin shoulders. I could feel the blades and I realized why they were named after a weapon. "I'm so sorry, Mom. We'll be okay. You'll get better work."

The tears fell freely then and she shook her head so that her hair covered her face. I noticed that the ends were frayed and a few wiry gray hairs popped up at the roots; she must not have seen her stylist in months.

I sat down next to her, my body suddenly heavy, like a packet of ground meat.

"I didn't want to upset you. I haven't paid the mortgage in months. I thought I'd be able to catch up, but the bank is going to foreclose. They won't negotiate. And now I get fired! It's too much. It's too much for one person."

She was sobbing, not even trying to hide it from me. I'd never seen her like this. I was an in vitro baby, born to a single mother who had never depended on a man. All she told me about my father was that he was over six feet tall, full-blooded Cherokee, and had a master's degree in psychology. My mom had wanted a baby and so she paid for a sperm donor and got pregnant. She'd never said anything was too much for her to handle. But we'd always had my grandma. Even when things weren't great, when I was lonely or felt bad about myself, I always had my grandma, my mom, and this house—my light-dappled bedroom, my cool-sheeted bed, the joyful trees. Coming home after another day at school to the scent of fresh herbs and lemons. My grandmother waiting with poetry and pastries. I wanted to tie myself to the door of the house so that the bank would have to let us stay. I couldn't stand the idea of another loss.

CLARK

2

My mom and I rented a two-bedroom apartment in the southern, not-so-fancy end of Beverly Hills because my mom liked the school district. I didn't mind changing schools; I didn't have any close friends at Hollywood High and I was going to graduate in a year anyway. I had been thinking more about my college applications to Stanford and UC Berkeley as a psychology major than about the fun I'd have senior year. But I hated the apartment, which was rundown and too small for most of our things. When we moved, we hauled off boxes to Goodwill and Out of the Closet. We got rid of most of my grandmother's possessions as well. China plates with roses and gold trim, china figurines, glass snow globes, table fountains with miniature gardens, heart-shaped cloisonné boxes full of hairpins, collections of paper clips and rubber bands, classical and world music CDs, yoga DVDs, books and books and books. Most everything we touched, if we paused to think about it, made us cry, so we sent it away quickly, without thinking. I really only kept the family photographs, some poetry books (Keats, Whitman, the Barrett-Brownings, Donne, and Dickinson of course), a bottle of Shalimar and a vial of lavender oil, the china lamp my grandmother had as a girl, and what was left of the vintage clothing and jewelry; there wasn't much—she'd given most of it to me already and my small closet was stuffed to overflowing.

Our first night in the apartment I was putting sweaters away when I came across something in one of the built-in drawers in my bedroom.

It was an old Ouija board. Perhaps the former tenant had left it behind.

I'd never had one as a kid; my mom, in spite of, or maybe because of, her writerly interest in the supernatural, said they creeped her out. "What if it works but it brings something unwanted back?" I'd heard her asking my grandmother once. I had always liked ghost stories and my mother's TV episodes about spirits. The supernatural intrigued me, but I didn't spend too much time thinking about it. Now my interest was piqued.

I examined the Ouija board in my hands. It had

old-fashioned, embellished black lettering arcing across the shiny light-gold-colored surface, a smiling sun, a sinister moon, shadowy, long-fingered people playing with their own board in the lower corners, and the ominous words GOOD BYE written on the bottom. I imagined the heart-dropping sensation you would experience if the marker on the board swept down to those words before your question had been answered.

On the other hand, what if the Ouija board *did* answer your question? People used them to communicate with the dead, didn't they? With spirits? Could I possibly connect to my grandmother this way? Could I learn what she'd wanted to tell me? Maybe I'd found the Ouija board for a reason.

Almost as soon as I'd had the thoughts, I dismissed them. For one thing, I didn't believe in ghosts. Did I? And if ghosts were real, what if "something unwanted" came? Maybe my mom's reaction from years before was influencing me or maybe I was just feeling the cool breeze coming through the windows, but I shivered from the nape of my neck to my tailbone. I put the Ouija board in my closet, hoping to forget about it, but at the same time, not quite ready to throw it away.

That night I left my grandma's lamp on. It was a china statue of a little girl standing on tiptoe to blow out a large candle, the flame of which was the lightbulb.

But the lamplight wasn't comforting and the air felt hot and close. Giving up on sleep, I went and got the urn of ashes from the living room. It was cool and heavy in my hands as I knelt by the bed, eyes closed, praying to Grandma Miriam to help me rest and to visit me in my dreams.

The prayer didn't work; I couldn't remember anything in the morning. It just felt as if I'd been pummeled by invisible fists all night and hadn't really slept. Every sound made me cringe—the dogs in the alley, the neighbor clicking around in high heels upstairs, a siren going by. I squinted out the window with over-sensitized, sleep-deprived eyes at the too-bright light in the palm trees and felt cold in the space between my ribs, as if I were holding my grandmother in my arms, waiting again for the ambulance to come. I wanted to hide from the world.

But I couldn't hide. It was both my first day at Beverly Hills High and the first day of the semester. B.H.H.S. was a public school, but it looked like a private academy; the lawn was spread out in a vast green carpet before the white, red-roofed, French Normandy-style buildings. As I walked past the pink-flowering trees and up the crowded front steps, I kept my head down and tried to be as invisible as possible in my black cashmere sweater and trousers. I wasn't exactly popular at Hollywood High, but I fit in better there among the geeks and punks than here, where there was so much wealth and beauty you felt like you were in a skin-care or sneaker commercial. Many celebrities had attended these hallowed halls, including Angelina Jolie and Lenny Kravitz, and movies from *It's a Wonderful Life* to *Clueless* had been filmed on its campus. In the first film, Jimmy Stewart and Donna Reed had jitterbugged into the Olympic-sized pool, built under the gym's sliding floor, and started a dance riot. I had much simpler aspirations; I just wanted to survive the first week.

In my math class, the teacher Mr. Mandelbaum's voice droned on and on, and I had to struggle to keep my eyes from closing, although I could usually concentrate pretty well in class. Just as I was losing the fight, a hand touched my arm.

At first I couldn't see who it was because of the bright green light flooding my vision, the color of the lawn of our old house in the afternoon sun. Was the sun in my eyes now? I blinked.

The boy next to me gave me a snaggletoothed smile. There was something disarming about that smile, something almost audacious about its lack of self-consciousness. His cheeks were flushed and he wore glasses like mine, and a *Buffy the Vampire Slayer* T-shirt.

What a geek, I thought affectionately.

"Don't fall asleep yet," he whispered. "It's only the first day."

"Thanks."

"Nice glasses."

"Yours, too."

On the way out, a blond girl passed us in the hall and I recognized her as Ally Kellogg from fifth grade. She had moved away for middle school, but I didn't know where she'd gone.

"Hi, Julie?" she said. I was shocked that she recognized me. "You go here now?"

I nodded.

She tossed me a "Cool, see you" and hurried off.

I expected the boy in the glasses to turn his head and forget about me, but he didn't seem to notice her at all. Instead he flashed me that grin, and ambled down the hallway.

He was in my health class as well, and as I ate my lunch in the quad, he came over and asked if he could sit with me.

"Your hat sort of reminds me of a moose," I said as he took a seat on the cement bench and brought a large ceramic pot out of his backpack. The headdress in question was brown wool with long earflaps.

"Thanks!" he replied as if I'd complimented him, which I guess I had, in a way. He made a cute moose. "I was going to wear this hat that's a wool monkey, but my mom thought it was too weird for my first day." His voice was kind of high and young sounding.

"Yeah. She was probably right. You might have to work up to that one."

Three cheerleaders approached a nearby bench. He smiled at them and waved, and they moved away to sit somewhere else.

"I'm not even wearing my monkey hat," he said.

"Maybe you just scared the cheerleaders with your smile?" I offered.

"Or my *kicharee*."

What?

He lifted the lid off the pot in front of him. A rich, savory smell came out of it. "An Indian dish of grains and beans. I made this one from brown rice and vegetables and coconut oil with spices. It's very healing. Want some?"

"No thanks. You carry that big thing around all day?"

He nodded at my metal Munsters lunch box. I hadn't touched the sandwich inside it yet. "I wouldn't talk," he said.

In spite of my desire to be invisible at this school, I hadn't been able to give up my lunch box. "It's retro and kitsch."

"Well, homemade vegan dining is the food of the future," he explained. "And not only that. I don't get why people think smiling is weird. Is smiling weird?"

I shrugged. "Not really, in and of itself, smiling isn't weird."

"But you'd think people would like you if you smile at them. It's better than frowning. Or, let's say, spitting."

"It is better than spitting, I'd agree."

"I'm kind of doing an experiment about why people are uncomfortable with self-expression. Especially in high school."

A group of boys in basketball jerseys walked by and he flashed the same grin ostentatiously at them. They ignored him, thank God.

"Is it an experiment in self-expression or masochism?" I asked.

"You're funny. I'm trying to see if it's regionally influenced."

"Where are you from?"

"Chicago."

"Why did you move here? Just to experiment?"

He tapped his fingers on the tabletop. His nails were gnawed down and his cuticles raw, which, in contrast to his easygoing manner, surprised me, though he wasn't smiling now. "My family wanted a change."

"How'd that monkey hat go over in Chicago?"

He grinned again, and I felt an odd, unexpected sense of relief. "Not bad. It's cold there, so . . ."

"So everyone needs a hat."

"Yeah. And I think people might be nicer in places

where it's cold because they have to coexist more. Don't get me wrong; I don't miss the cold. I've stored enough cold in my bones forever. But they have something to bond over besides their favorite *Buffy the Vampire Slayer* episodes or whatever."

I nodded at his shirt. "You're into *Buffy*?"

"I know," he said. "I'm a total nerd."

"Me too, then, I guess. Joss Whedon is pure genius!"

"What's your favorite episode?" he asked me.

I didn't have to think long. "Where her mom dies. The way they don't use any music for the whole episode."

"It's so much scarier than any monster," he said. "Death, you know?"

We didn't speak. I slid back the ruby-studded skirt of my grandmother's silver lady-shaped watch pin to reveal the time. Lunch was almost over.

"Hey, I'm Clark." His hands were big and he had a good grip when we shook. I felt badly that I hadn't paid attention when his name was called in class, especially when he said, "You're Julie. Some of us were actually awake in math."

BY MY LAST PERIOD, I had a second wind of energy, maybe because it was AP English. The teacher, Ms. Merritt, looked like Emily Dickinson with her brown hair in a bun, her buttoned-up blouse, and small, bird body. There were

portraits of famous authors all over the walls and a corner
reading area with a bookcase full of leather-bound volumes,
a big leather arm chair, and a Tiffany lamp. I liked her right
away.

"We'll be studying a lot of poetry this term," she said,
"and we're going to start by writing an in-class essay about
your relationship to poetry in your life so far."

Everyone grumbled, but I thought of my grandmother
and knew there was at least one place at school where I'd
belong, besides at lunch with the nerd-of-all-nerd boys.

WHEN I GOT HOME from school, my mom was curled up on
the couch in a fetal position wearing her pajamas.

"What's wrong?" I asked. Her face looked pinched, and
there were shadows under her eyes like she'd applied smoky
makeup upside down.

"Everything is fine, really. I just have my period." But
I knew she was upset about her job and the house and my
grandmother. How could I be honest about the strange things
that happened since Grandma Miriam died, when my mom
couldn't even admit what was really going on with her?

I went to get her something to eat, but when I opened the
refrigerator, there was nothing except some expired milk,
a jar of pickles, and ketchup. Either my mom didn't have
enough money for groceries or she was just too depressed

to go shopping, which wasn't exactly a consolation. I threw out the milk, got a plate of crackers for each of us, and then went to my room. She didn't even ask me how my first day of school was.

That night, unable to sleep, I got up to get a glass of water. My mom was at the kitchen table on her laptop; when she saw me, she minimized her screen.

"What?" I said.

"What what?"

"What are you doing?"

"Looking for a job. Why are you freaking out, Julie?"

"You shut off the computer when I came in."

She swiveled her chair around to glare at me. "So what?"

"Mom!" I said. "What's going on? Don't lie to me. Whatever it is . . ."

My mother sighed and touched the keyboard so the screen lit back up. There was a dating website on there. Her picture, self-snapped, smiling, wearing too much makeup, looking expectant and vulnerable. GHOSTWRITER/F/SINGLE/48/ BEVERLY HILLS, CALIFORNIA.

"I need to have a life," she said.

Then get a job, I thought, but it was too mean to say out loud.

"I'm too dependent on you. What happens when you start going out with boys?" she went on.

This made me almost wish I'd cut her off with the job comment when I had had the chance. "I don't want to go out with anyone. There isn't anybody I like that way."

"How about him for me?" she said. I guess she hadn't really been listening. She was suppressing a smile as she clicked on a thumbnail of a man with long, black hair, blue eyes, and a cleft in his chin. DESCENTMAN/M/S/41/LOS ANGE-LES, CALIFORNIA.

"Too young," I said.

"See, I knew I shouldn't have showed you." She looked sad again and I wished I hadn't been so negative.

"He's kind of good-looking. What does he do?"

"He has a band," she said, and my negativity unapologetically returned.

"A band? What is he, seventeen?"

"Mick Jagger was born in '43," she said.

What? I didn't see how that applied. "Does he have a day job?"

"I don't know," said my mom over the scream of an ambulance siren going by outside. "I have to meet him and find out."

I couldn't even have a real conversation with her about guys. How could I share anything serious with her even if I'd wanted to? She had never seemed so far away from me.

THE NEXT DAY IT was hard to get out of bed—my muscles felt dense and heavy, rigid as bones. It was pouring rain. I pulled the covers over my head to muffle the excruciating clamor of the drops on the thin roof of our apartment building. When I finally got up, there was a small puddle on the floor. I put a pan under the leak and went to tell my mom, but she was sleeping. I remembered when she used to make me waffles and bacon and scrambled eggs and fresh-squeezed orange juice for breakfast and we'd sit at the kitchen table in the old house and talk about our dreams from the night before and what the day would hold. Since my grandma died, I had cornflakes by myself almost every morning and sometimes for dinner. The thought of pouring the cold milk on the cold cornflakes made me want to bury myself back in bed. I could have stayed there all day; it had been another rough night of restless sleep.

I couldn't find an umbrella, so my grandmother's old leopard-print coat was drenched by the time I got to school (why had I worn it?), and I was late. I saw a tall person run toward me up the big front steps. His glasses were spattered like windshields in spite of the big yellow umbrella he was carrying. And he was wearing the monkey hat in spite of my discouraging remarks.

"Hey."

"Hi, Clark."

"You remembered my name. Awesome. I overslept."

"Me too."

"Care to share my umbrella-ella-ella?"

I ducked gratefully under it with him in spite of the bad Rihanna imitation. I could smell the spices from his *kicharee* coming out of his backpack. He was smiling.

IN HEALTH CLASS, MR. Roston had us pick partners for a project. As I watched everyone pair off, Clark tapped my shoulder. I was relieved not to have to endure the rejection of a roomful of strangers any longer and nodded at him. The teacher handed out a list of topics for us to choose from.

"How about 'sudden cardiac arrest'?" I said, looking it over, thinking of my grandmother, of course, then immediately wondering why I would want to do a project that would upset me so much.

"I'd like to do it on teens killed in drunk-driving accidents," said Clark.

I pulled my sleeves down over my hands as an inordinately powerful chill shook my shoulder blades. Maybe it was because my sweater was still damp from the rain or maybe I was freaked out by the idea of teens killed in drunk-driving accidents. But I was glad to have a topic that didn't make me think of my grandma's death. This boy had made me grateful three times in one day and it wasn't even lunchtime yet.

At the end of English, Ms. Merritt took me aside. "I read your essay about poetry, Julie. I really liked how you wrote about the way your grandmother introduced it to you."

I thanked her without meeting her gaze because I was afraid my eyes would tear up at the mention of Grandma Miriam.

"You have a lot of talent for writing and your test scores are very high. Have you already thought about where you'll be applying to school next year?"

I told her Stanford and Cal, in psychology. "But I don't think I can afford them." I didn't add that I was worried about my mom being able to buy groceries.

"Those are great choices. And there's financial aid available. You should get the applications online." She looked at me closely, reading my face like a poem. "Please let me know if I can help you out at all."

The kindness in her voice made my throat constrict under the necklace of my grandmother's pearls and I wanted to get out of there before I really started crying.

The following day after school, Clark came over to my apartment wearing a porkpie hat. My mom smiled at me in an annoying way as she shook his hand. She might as well have winked when I said we'd be in my room. Ugh.

I asked if he was hungry, although all I had to offer was cold cereal or peanut butter sandwiches. But Clark took out his warm ceramic pot of *kicharee* from the insulated backpack, and we shared what was left over from lunch. It was surprisingly delicious, maybe more so because I hadn't eaten a real home-cooked meal in a while.

"Wow, you're so healthy," I said, scraping my bowl. "Do you plan on living forever?"

"I didn't always used to be this neurotic. If that's what you want to call it. But shit happens, and if the worst thing I do in response is only eat *kicharee*, then, cool."

"What about when you can't cook?" I asked him.

"I'll eat regular food if I have to. But I'm kind of scared that when I go to college they'll force me to eat dorm food and then I may die from hydrogenated oils and artificial dyes."

I asked where he wanted to go, if food wasn't an issue.

"I'd like to get in to MIT," he said. "If I can keep my grades up. How about you?"

I told him what Ms. Merritt had said about financial aid for Stanford and Cal.

"In that case we should print the forms for you now. Then we can watch *Buffy*."

So after I downloaded the applications for my dream schools, we got serious. He sprawled himself out on the floor, I sat against the bed, and we watched the *Buffy the Vampire Slayer* episode where Willow and Tara make the rose levitate.

"Now that is great television," I said.

"They are by far my favorite couple on this show," Clark added in a somber tone as if he was discussing a very important matter. "And Whedon creates the perfect metaphor for their budding sexual relationship."

This raised him even further in my estimation.

Next we watched "I Only Have Eyes for You," in which the ghost of a dead high school student, who killed the teacher he was having an affair with, possesses Buffy. I didn't enjoy the episode as much as I usually did because it made me recall the Ouija board in my closet.

"Do you believe in ghosts?" Clark's voice was soft but it startled me; the show had affected my nerves. I couldn't see his eyes under the brim of his hat in the darkening room.

"I don't know," I said. "Do you?"

He shrugged.

"Sometimes I wish they were real," I surprised myself by saying. "Since my grandma died."

I told Clark the story of Grandma Miriam's death, leaving out the lavender light and the music but including the last words she'd said. Then I told him how my mom lost the house, that we had to move, and about how I'd found the Ouija board in the new apartment.

He was so quiet, I wished I hadn't told him. I couldn't afford to scare off my only friend.

"Sorry," I said. "Does that freak you out?"

I could see his Adam's apple move. "Not per se."

"What does that mean?"

He paused. "I guess it sort of does. Anything to do with ghosts. I mean real stuff. Not TV or books."

"So I guess that means you believe in them," I said.

"Shouldn't we work on our report?" said Clark. "It's getting kind of late."

And, to both our relief, I guess, the conversation was closed.

THAT WEEKEND MY MOM put on a push-up bra, a bright red halter top, tight jeans, and black patent-leather heels. She had trimmed and dyed her hair herself, and although she looked better, it seemed as if she was trying too hard and it bothered me that she was doing this for a guy she hadn't even met yet. Also, she was wearing my grandmother's Shalimar—citrus, flowers, and vanilla turned to amber liquid in a bottle that looked like a genie could come out of it. We kept the bottle on the mantel of the fake fireplace, beside Grandma's ashes; as far as I was concerned the perfume was sacred, not something to be worn on a first internet date.

I grunted at my mother when she tried to kiss me good-bye.

"Don't be mad, baby," she said. "Maybe you want to invite Clark over?"

"Mom! Don't say it like that!"

"Like what?" She batted her curled eyelashes.

"Like, all cute. He's just my friend. Whom I actually know. Unlike this person you're going out with."

"I'm going to find out who he is."

"He could be anybody. Aren't you supposed to meet him for coffee during the day first?"

"It's just one drink. I'll be back soon. You can call my cell if you need anything."

"I'm fine. It's you I'm worried about." I wanted to say that she was acting like a stupid teenager and dressing like a hooker, but I bit the fleshy inside of my lip and kept quiet. My grandmother would have understood. If she were here, I was sure my mom wouldn't be dating some stranger from the internet. It made me miss Grandma Miriam more, especially when I smelled her perfume on my mom's neck.

"You're wearing the Shalimar."

"So?" my mom said.

"You act like you don't even care that she's gone." I slammed down *Wuthering Heights*.

My mother sat on the couch next to me and I got another

whiff of the perfume. It made me sick to think of Descent-man smelling it on her neck. "Of course I do," she said.

Then why don't you talk about her? I wanted to shout. *Why don't you ask me? I was there when she died and you've never asked me about the moment of her death.* My mom hadn't brought it up after our first brief discussion. I was suddenly rigid with anger at being unable to tell her what I had seen and heard when my grandma died, even though it had been my choice to keep it a secret at the time.

Of course my mom wasn't aware of all the questions in my mind. She was still defending herself from the one accusation I had verbalized. "I just need something to help me forget. I sit around all day thinking about her."

"Don't!" I said. "Go out and get a job."

"I'm trying," she told me, and I knew by her shaky voice and the way she fanned her face to hold back mascara-wrecking tears, that I had pushed too far.

Then she left me sitting by the window, looking down at the palm trees and cars and people with good hair heading out for their Friday night dates. Usually she would have stayed to talk things out if we had an argument, but now it seemed like she just wanted to get away from me, to see some guy she hardly knew. That was when I realized how bad things were between us.

To numb my anger and my guilt at being so harsh with

her, I watched a Japanese movie about ghosts and ate a whole frozen pizza and a pint of frozen yogurt. Maybe it was the movie or too much dairy or sugar or the argument with my mom, but every sound seemed magnified ten times and made me jump.

Alone in the apartment at night for the first time, I wanted to talk to my grandmother, to feel her stroke my hair and call me her turtle dove.

In that moment after she died, she was more intensely with me than she had ever been before. But now there was no lavender light, no strange music, not even any dreams. Only a cold longing.

A heavy stillness in the apartment made it hard to breathe so I got up and opened a window. The night air smelled of car exhaust and the intimations of rain, and I heard a siren in the distance. It seemed I was always hearing sirens, ever since the only one that really mattered had left, carrying Grandma Miriam away from us.

I regretted, then, how my mother and I had gotten rid of so many of my grandmother's things, unable to face the pins that had held up her hair, the dishes on which she had eaten. There were only the photo albums that I kept under my bed, and the jewelry, shoes, and clothes. I was wearing her red satin kimono and I stroked the sleeve. The skin on my fingers was dry, and the material caught and snagged.

I got her photo album from under my bed frame. There were pictures of my grandmother as a chubby, towheaded baby, grinning in white lace, and as a young girl. Those green eyes that seemed to glow in the black-and-white shots. There were pictures of her at family functions, relatives I didn't recognize leaning in around a table, my grandmother in the middle, smiling brightest of anyone. A beaming, over-posed graduation portrait. There were wedding pictures of her with my grandfather, Maury. She and my grandfather both looked stiff and self-conscious but happy, Grandma Miriam in a white taffeta dress that showed off her shapely legs and a short, neat veil. In the honeymoon pictures taken in Hawaii, she absolutely shone—pure, curvy, vintage beauty with a hibiscus flower behind her ear. Her first secretarial job in a tailored tweed suit with a gardenia pinned to the lapel. The pictures of my mother as a baby, her father holding her up to the light from a window in their Brooklyn brownstone. Maury and Miriam and my mom on a vacation in Hollywood, posed in front of the Chinese theater.

After that trip they moved to Los Angeles and lived in a Santa Monica bungalow until Grandpa Maury died. There was a picture of Mom in her twenties at a dinner in a new black dress with shoulder pads, and bad '80s poodle hair, celebrating her first writing job. There she was with better hair and a better outfit, looking happy and pregnant. The photo album ended with a baby picture of me.

Wanting more of my grandmother, I went to her glass-topped filigree jewelry box on my bureau. The rose satin-lined interior was full of tangled strands of pearls and chains, rhinestones and shell cameos as well as the silver and turquoise and chunks of amber she wore later in her life. I stacked my arms with some mother-of-pearl bangles and a silver cuff in the shape of a calla lily and hung a delicate silver cobweb necklace, studded with pearl dewdrops, around my neck. Lastly I pinned the silver watch shaped like a lady to my kimono.

My grandmother's voice came to me again in that moment: *There's something I must tell you.*

What had she wanted to say? I wished with a deep pang in the empty jewel box of my heart that I could go to find her, wherever she was, and ask her.

Then I heard something fall inside my closet, a small and sudden disruption with no obvious cause. I opened the door to see. The Ouija board box had toppled onto the floor.

I got it out of the closet and set the board on my knees. It was only a child's toy, but maybe it was something more. Again I wondered why the Ouija board had been left in our apartment in the first place. In my room as if for me to find. And it had fallen at exactly the right moment as if someone was trying to tell me something. If Ouija boards could really help you communicate with the spirit world, there was only one person I wanted to reach.

I rested my fingers lightly on top of the marker that was shaped a little like a heart. I held my breath and let my hands skate across the board's surface, pulled by some unseen force. "Grandma," I whispered to the air. "Miriam. Miriam Klein?"

The marker looped and skidded around the board, not stopping anywhere, until it slid off and landed on the floor.

There was no answer and I felt silly for trying.

AROUND MIDNIGHT I WOKE to the sound of my mom's car, as if I had been listening for it in my sleep, and went to the window. I watched her parallel park. It took her a few times. Behind her car was a truck. The internet guy got out.

He followed her to the front door. I covered my head with a pillow and squeezed my eyes shut like a child trying to make herself disappear.

MY MOM WAS LIKE a different person after her date with "Descentman," aka Luke. There were scrambled eggs or pancakes for breakfast and hot meals for dinner for a week. She got dressed every morning and sat down to peruse the want ads online. Luke took her out to dinner and a movie two weekends in a row and she came home flushed and literally beaming. But I still didn't like the idea of this virtual stranger. She hadn't had a boyfriend since before I was born, and I knew it was important, but who was Luke? *Maybe I am just jealous of him,* I thought guiltily. I missed the takeout and foreign film nights with my mom more than ever.

I told Clark at school, but all he said was, "At least she's happy." Which wasn't helpful at all. But he must have known I needed a little more support than that because the next day at lunchtime he handed me a CD he'd burned.

"What's this?" I asked.

"Just some music I thought you'd like." Arcade Fire, The White Stripes, Radiohead, Adele, The Kills, Pixies, Breeders, Smashing Pumpkins.

He really was a pretty cool guy. I thanked him, touching his arm, and he blushed, the color rising up from his jawline.

Luckily I had him. For the next few weeks we ate his *kicharee* together every day in the quad and he came over almost every afternoon. We listened to music, watched *Buffy*, and studied.

Sometimes we walked to the library instead. The Beverly Hills Public Library was a large, white, red-roofed building like the high school. Palm trees flanked the entrance, and leaded-glass windows lit the interior with sun. Clark liked to read about as much as I did, but he preferred writers like

Edgar Allan Poe, H. P. Lovecraft, Clive Barker, and Stephen King.

"I don't get why you like that stuff but you don't like to talk about Ouija boards," I whispered to him one day as we sat across from each other at the table, sharing the light from a reading lamp.

"I told you, it's different when it's not real," he whispered back.

"So you think Ouija boards can really summon the dead?"

Clark adjusted his glasses on his nose. "I don't know. There's something about them that just seems wrong to me." He shrugged. "Sorry, I'm a wimp."

"A very cool one. With great taste in music. I listen to that CD all the time."

"I figured you could use something to take your mind off things," he said. "Music's usually kind of great for that."

I ESPECIALLY NEEDED TO have my mind taken off things when I met Luke that night. I was sitting up in the living room reading *Anna Karenina* when they came in. He wore all black and had shoulder-length hair that looked as if it had been dyed to match his outfit.

When my mom introduced us, he shook my hand. His grip was weak and his palm felt clammy. "Well, I better get going. Just wanted to say hello." Even from where I stood, his breath smelled of alcohol.

"Are you sure you don't want to stay for a drink?" my mom said.

I couldn't believe she was actually asking for him to stay when I was sitting right there. I tried to give her the evil eye, but she ignored me; she was gazing at Luke.

"Next time, beautiful Rachel." He kissed her cheek and I heard the sound of his saliva.

My stomach lurched. Outside, as if on cue, the storm that had been threatening poured from the clouds.

I went to my room to shut out the rain of my thoughts with Clark's music.

"UGH, I FINALLY MET the boyfriend," I told him the next day at school.

"What's he like?"

"Aging rocker dude with a dead-fish handshake."

"Sounds bad. Have you been playing lots of music?"

"I think this is something even your music mixes can't help," I said.

Clark bit his lip and tapped his knuckles against his chin. "Well then, I think you need something else."

So, after school he took me to a secondhand clothing shop on Pico I'd never been to before.

"We can find you appropriate attire for when you become a famous psychologist with a degree from Stanford," Clark told me, leading the way inside.

Treasure Hunt smelled mothball-woolly and musty and was jammed with cool stuff—furniture, lamps, tchotchkes, books, accessories, and clothes. A small back room with a round rack held extra-special finds. I was riffling through the dresses when one of my grandmother's cameo rings caught on a lilac lace gown. I carefully unsnagged it and held the dress out to get a better look. Clark heard me gasp and came over, wearing a fedora with a small, tattered feather in the brim and carrying some clothes over his arm.

"What's wrong?"

"This looks just like one of her dresses," I said.

"Whose?"

"My grandma. Miriam." It was the first time I'd mentioned her to him since he'd come over to watch *Buffy*. "I mean, it's the same dress."

He frowned at the lace draped in my hands. "Did you give it away?"

"I didn't think so. I remember it from when I was little. I used to try it on. We would never have given it . . ."

"Well, maybe she did?"

I shook my head. "I don't think so."

"Maybe it's a different one?" Clark offered. "Maybe you have the other one at home?"

"I don't remember seeing it lately," I told him. I checked the label, remembering the gold lettering: MADEMOISELLE DENTELLE.

An elderly saleslady with rhinestone-studded eyeglasses and unmistakably blue hair came over to ask if we needed help. She looked at us suspiciously, and Clark grinned back at her. "We were wondering if you know where this dress came from?" he said.

"I have no idea," she replied with a sniff that implied we smelled like unwashed used clothing.

"Well, we'd like to buy it," he told her.

Clark got a Led Zeppelin T-shirt, a wool argyle old-man sweater, and a tie, and he bought me the mysterious dress, although I tried to argue with him and pay for it myself. Perhaps I imagined it, but I could smell Shalimar wafting from its fabric. I had no idea if it was the same dress or not or how it had gotten there, but I held it against my heart, thinking of my grandmother. I thanked Clark and considered kissing his cheek but decided against it to keep from embarrassing him.

When we left I noticed a HELP WANTED sign in the window among the mannequins dressed in recycled Halloween costumes, and asked Clark if he minded if I went back inside. The saleslady (and owner), whose name was Mrs. Carol, was more friendly after we'd made an actual purchase and handed me an application that I filled out right there, with Clark's encouragement. I knew I needed a job to take my mind off things, not to mention make some spending money, since I couldn't depend on my mother for much anymore. And the dress, whether it was my grandmother's or an exact replica, felt like a sign.

Clark walked me home in the lavender-tinged, dinner-scented air and right to my front door, but I didn't ask him in.

I wish I had.

Luke was in the kitchen, heating up a bowl of beans in the microwave.

"Hello," he said calmly. "Julie. How are you?"

I stared at him in the harsh light that showed off the faded acne scars on his cheeks; he looked as relaxed in my kitchen as if he lived with us. I couldn't believe that he was in there at all without my mother. How long had they been seeing each other, five minutes?

"You don't look okay," he said, and I felt my back bristle like a cat's. How did he know what was okay for me or not?

"Where's my mom?" I clutched the dress closer to me.

"Your mother wasn't feeling well." Luke took the beans

out of the microwave. The smell made me gag. "She asked me to come over and make her something to eat."

I headed toward her bedroom and he called me back. "She's sleeping. Let her sleep. She's had a hard week."

So have I.

But I didn't go to her room.

I lay down on my bed in my clothes, thinking about my mother and this stranger in her room together. The walls in the apartment were thin; I might hear something I really didn't want to.

So I put on my headphones and blasted the CD Clark made me, trying to chase any thoughts out of my head. "Ready to Start" was so loud and encompassing with its driving beat and urgent vocals that I didn't hear my phone ring, but I felt it vibrate; it was Clark.

"Hey," he said. "I was just checking up on you."

Through the walls I could hear my mom and Luke listening to heavy metal.

Metal, really? My mom was suddenly a metal fan?

"Luke's here," I said.

"The creepy boyfriend?"

"Yeah. I don't get why my mom's dating him. She must be having some kind of midlife crisis." I wasn't the type to think about being rescued by a boy—it wasn't my thing—but all of a sudden I wanted Clark to ask me how he could help.

"You should come by," I said.

"It's late, and I have a report due Monday," said Clark, and I was surprised that I felt disappointment, and a little irritated with him for not coming anyway. This didn't really make sense; it wasn't like I had a crush on him or anything.

"But maybe Wednesday," he added after my disappointed, irritated pause. "Right after school? We can walk home and do some Halloween stuff if you want. I'll wear a hat."

"Of course you will," I said, softening, smiling into the receiver. "But come around four thirty. I need time to get ready."

IN THE MORNING, AFTER Luke left, I went into my mom's bedroom, holding the lace dress. I'd decided to ask her about it. Maybe she had given it away for some reason.

"Can I talk to you?"

"Sure, sweetie."

I sat at the end of the bed, not wanting to get too close to her; I could still feel Luke's presence in the room. It was dark except for a sliver of light through the blinds, so I put on the lamp and she shielded her eyes and gasped.

"I found this in a secondhand store," I said, ignoring her reaction.

She sat up and blinked at the dress in my hands. "Oh, it's lovely."

"Do you recognize it?"

She shook her head.

"It was Grandma's."

"I don't think so, Julie," my mom said. "We kept all of her clothes. That's why your closet is such a mess. It must be a look-alike."

"No, it's not in there." I had checked the night before.

"I really don't know then. But I need to get some more sleep. Can we talk about this later?"

I was pretty sure that wouldn't happen but it didn't matter. At least I had the dress.

And a job at the store where I'd found it. Mrs. Carol hired me at Treasure Hunt and set me to work doing displays on the first day. I loved being around all the old dresses although I worried that I'd spend my paychecks on them. Before I left that night, I asked Mrs. Carol about the lace dress again, if she remembered how she got it, but she only said, "Some dresses are like people, Julie. They feel very familiar right away, not because you've had them in your life before but because you are supposed to have them in your life."

Wow, I thought, *she's a master salesperson.*

"Kind of like that young man you were with," Mrs. Carol added, busying herself with the cash register and not looking at me. "I bet you felt like you knew him when you met."

Clark? No, not really.

She must have read my expression. "He's special. You'll see it eventually even if you don't now. Why is it that girls have to grow up to appreciate the really good ones?"

LATE AUTUMN LIGHT FELL in through the windows, cold-white radiance, reminding me of winter. My mother slept in her room and she hadn't gotten up all day; I wondered if she was going back to the pre-Luke behavior. It was Halloween, and the air smelled vaguely of smoke and sounded like the crunch of dried leaves. I had carved a small pumpkin and bought a bag of candy bars, but I knew no trick-or-treaters would come upstairs to our apartment. The manager made us keep the lobby door locked and refused to put up any welcoming decorations.

When I buzzed Clark in and opened the door, he blushed and smiled like he was going to say something complimentary about my lilac lace dress, but then just tipped the top hat he'd worn to school that day ("the only day of the year I can dress like myself and not seem weird") and I was surprised to realize I was a little disappointed. I didn't think I cared that much about what he thought.

We didn't talk a lot, just went into my room to eat some

candy and watch the *Buffy* Halloween episodes.

But then, before we'd even started, I heard a clatter from my closet.

I popped up and opened the closet door.

The Ouija board fell out.

Again?

"It's Halloween, too," Clark said, tugging at the pink-and-black tie he'd purchased at the thrift store. "That's pretty weird."

I fingered the slightly rough lace skirt of my dress. "Everything's been so weird. It seems like a sign or something."

Clark held his chin in his hand, digging his fingers so hard I wondered if it hurt. "What kind of sign?"

"From my grandmother?" I was immediately embarrassed and added, "I don't know."

"You want to use it to reach her?"

I didn't have to respond; he could probably see my answer written in the air between us, in ornate Ouija board lettering.

"Okay," he said. "If you need to."

"You don't sound so sure."

"I want to help you, Julie."

I had an impulse to hug him but instead I said, "We need more chocolate for this," and handed him a miniature candy bar, then taking one for myself.

He blushed as if he'd read my mind about the hug, or maybe it was the way I'd smiled when I gave him the chocolate.

I picked up the box, took the Ouija board out, and brought it over to where he sat on the floor.

We faced each other, knee to knee, the board between us, our fingers very close on the marker. He kept his cramped up like spiders so they could fit, as if he was afraid to touch me.

"I know this is weird," I said. "I hope it doesn't freak you out too much. I know you told me . . ."

His eyes were darting around the room but he said, "It's okay."

"I really miss her." The sudden tears made my eyes sting with makeup and I wondered if my mascara would run, then realized that Clark wouldn't care about something like that. Even though I wished he had complimented my dress, it was nice not having to worry about impressing him.

He nodded. "I understand. Believe me."

The relief at this response expanded like a breath in my chest and I wanted to tell him more. "I've thought about going after her," I said.

I expected him to look confused or shocked if he got what I meant, but instead he said, "That makes sense to me."

We both looked down at the marker. There was a breathlessness in the room, in the air.

I forced my lungs to take in more oxygen; there never felt like quite enough in that apartment, and it was more true than ever that night. "This is stupid." I wanted him to tell me it wasn't.

As if on cue he said, "No it's not. Let's try."

The sun was sinking and the room grew darker. "Miriam?" I said. "Grandma?"

And then the marker was moving and I wanted to take my hands away because suddenly they were shaking, but I kept them there.

"Are you here?" I asked, and the marker sped to YES.

My heart had legs; it was running away. "Are you Miriam?"

NO.

"Who are you?"

The marker went to the letter G.

Grandma, I thought.

R

A

N

But then Clark let go, so it slid back across the board to me.

He un-crumpled his long, gray corduroy legs awkwardly, like a foal learning to stand.

"I have to go," he said.

"Why?"

"I just do, okay? I'll see you later."

And then Clark ran, he literally ran, out of my apartment. I watched him through the window, holding his hat, taking off down the street of jack-o'-lanterns and plastic skeletons and little, screaming, bloody ghouls with pillowcase sacks, his legs flailing, almost stumbling, like he was trying to escape something or someone.

I picked up the Ouija board and tried by myself, but nothing happened. I was so mad at Clark for leaving at that moment, when my grandmother was about to come. G-R-A-N . . . Damn. I tried to call him but he didn't answer. So I ate the whole bag of candy, took off my grandmother's dress (it was too tight anyway; the zipper left a mark), and got into bed. Outside I could hear the cries of children and I remembered trick-or-treating with my mother and grandmother in the old neighborhood when I was a kid, wearing the elaborate costumes they had made for me, walking through hills that smelled of trees and bonfires, and coming home to sit on the floor and sort through my candy while the fire blazed in the hearth. My grandmother always prepared a big dinner of roast chicken and pumpkin soup and potatoes and green beans and salad before we went out, so I wouldn't get sick on sugar, she said.

But without her and her dinners and her love, my

candy-belly hurt and I lay facedown on the sheets, thinking about my skittish friend, my absent or sleeping mother, my grandmother who had been so close and now was as gone as she had ever been.

I lay there with my grandmother's urn and photo album, under the dream catcher she had given me when I was a child, wishing I could just pass out. Wishing that I could join my grandma wherever she was.

SHE SHOULD HAVE BEEN in my dream. I was in our old house, except that it was sitting on a body of water that reflected it on all sides. Reeds grew out of the water, and the air was foggy. I was walking from room to room, looking for my grandma. The rooms were empty and my voice echoed off the blank walls. My footsteps rang on the wooden floors. Where was she?

Something was tattooed on my arm in red ink, words I couldn't understand. When did I get a tattoo? I kept trying to read the words, but they looked upside down or backward or maybe in another language.

Then I was caught in a flashing red light that came through the window, and an alarm sounded and I was running, running, and then sinking into water, trying to get away from whomever it was that was going—on no uncertain terms, and with vile intent—to harm the shit out of me.

GRANT

3

At school the next day, Clark wasn't in health class, but I found him at lunch, in the quad, on what had become "our bench." His head was down and he didn't have his *kicharee* with him.

"What happened? Where'd you go?"

He glanced up at me and shrugged.

"She was so close, Clark. Why'd you leave when she was so close?" I tried to keep the resentment out of my voice but it didn't work. My nerves were frayed like the jeans Clark wore.

He ripped a piece of paper out of a notebook and began tearing it into small shreds and balling them up. "Look, Julie, I tried, but I'm not comfortable with that supernatural stuff, unless it's just entertainment, okay? I told you. I'm just not into it."

"Whatever. Okay, sorry. But you didn't have to leave like that. And not call me back. And then you weren't in class. . . ."

"I had a headache, okay?" He tossed one of the balled-up papers into a trash can; it missed. "Fuck," he said softly, and pulled the beret off his head, crushing it in his hand. "I can't even make a basket in a trash can?" He looked like he was about to cry.

My anger paled like a ghost next to his vivid frustration and, even though I still didn't really understand, I said, "It's okay, Clark. Forget about it. We don't have to use the Ouija board anymore." I took out some leftover Halloween candy and we stuffed our faces, not talking for the rest of the lunch period.

LATER THAT NIGHT I was trying to sleep, still amped on Halloween sugar and restless with anxiety from my dream the night before, when I heard a tapping at my window. I jumped up and then I just froze, standing there in the middle of my room in my mom's vintage Stooges T-shirt, unable to move or speak. Someone was calling from down below, "Julie!"

I crept over to the window and looked out. A boy was

standing in the alleyway next to my house. He was tall and lanky with dark hair. The red streetlight shone, reflected in a pool of water at his feet so that he seemed to glow with its color. I didn't recognize him at first without a hat on and because he wasn't posed in his usual slump.

"Clark?"

"Hi," he said. The streetlamps made a buzzing sound.

"Can I come up?"

I wriggled into the plaid skinny jeans that lay on the floor by the bed; for a second I almost stopped to put on a bra but I decided not to. It was just Clark. He probably wouldn't even notice.

He wasn't wearing his glasses and his hair was slicked back away from his face, showing off high cheekbones that had always been hidden before. He still wasn't smiling and looked completely different without the sloppy grin.

"How's it going?" he asked, standing in the doorway with his hands in his hoodie pockets.

"What'd you do, get a haircut or something?"

He didn't answer, but his eyes never left my face. They were big and dark, pupils dilated. "Can I come in?"

I locked the lobby door behind us and he followed me inside and up the stairs. His feet were so soundless that for a moment I had to look back to make sure he was still there.

We snuck into the apartment. My mom was on the

couch—she'd fallen asleep there and we had to tiptoe past her into my room. I sat on the bed. Clark lowered himself onto the floor, still watching my face.

"What's up?" I asked him. "Are you okay?"

"Julie?"

"Yeah? What's wrong? You're freaking me out here." I hugged my arms around my chest, suddenly wishing I'd put the bra on.

"Relax." He was still just staring at me, not smiling.

Clark would never say "Relax."

"Who are you?" I was only half joking. "What have you done with my friend?"

He cleared his throat and smoothed his hair down. It was a gesture I'd never seen Clark make. I felt a little sick.

"Okay," I said, extending the last syllable. "What's going on here?"

"Don't freak. I'm Clark's twin brother, Grant."

A brother had never been mentioned. I felt like I was in a *Buffy* episode. "What the hell? Stop messing with me!"

His eyes flickered for a moment down to my breasts; I had uncrossed my arms and I covered myself again. My heart was beating like I'd been running.

"Clark's told me a lot about you. He felt bad about leaving like that. He said you were really sad about your grandma."

I shook my head back and forth to clear it. "A twin?

Why didn't he tell me about you?" The more I stared at him, the more it seemed like he was telling the truth; they looked alike but not exactly. And their voices were different—Grant's was richer, deeper—and the way Grant's eyes almost glowed when they touched my body. . . . I should have known right away.

"Clark doesn't like to talk about me."

"Why not?"

"Sibling rivalry?" He smiled for the first time. Then he bent down and picked up the Ouija board box, rapping on it with his knuckles. "Is this how you tried to reach her?"

"What?"

"Your grandma. Is this how?"

I took the box away from him. "I still don't get why Clark didn't mention you," I said, exasperated.

"I was away for a while. I just got back. I guess I kind of hurt him. I didn't mean to. He's kind of shut down about the whole thing."

"Really shut down. He never said anything at all about a brother."

"It's a long story." There was something feline about the way he moved, leaning back on his elbows and crossing his long legs.

"Prove it," I said, surprising myself with the words.

"Prove what?"

"That you're not Clark. How do I know you're not messing with me?"

He got up from the floor and shook out his legs. He ran his fingers over his hair. It was like electric sparks were coming off him. He picked up the mix CD from Clark, turned it over in his hand, and then set it down again. "What do you want me to do?"

"Tell me something about Clark. That he wouldn't tell me himself."

"I can't betray the kid like that." Grant sucked in his cheeks, making the bones appear more prominent. "Although I guess *I'm* his best secret. In the flesh." There was the smile again, slow and symmetrical. Not Clark's grin.

"Why did you come here?" I asked.

Grant's gaze didn't waver. "Clark was really upset. He said he left and he felt bad about it. I know how much he likes you and I wanted to see if I could help."

I scowled at him. "So he doesn't know you came?"

"No. And we probably shouldn't tell him. I wasn't kidding about the sibling rivalry. I keep an eye out for the dude but I try to give him his space whenever possible."

"A lot of space. I've known him a couple of months and . . ."

"I graduated from Hancock in Chicago a year early and

I stayed there with our aunt. I just got back. Like I said, sometimes I think it freaks him out to have me around."

None of this sounded particularly reassuring. And I still had questions. "How'd you even know where I live?"

Grant shrugged. "We're brothers, remember. With cell phones. It wasn't hard."

Grant walked slowly over to me. An ambulance drove by, throwing a swath of light across the wall. It lit the boy up for a second so that his whole body had a red sheen to it.

Then Grant came and sat next to me on the bed. I could smell wood smoke and candy.

He leaned closer so I could feel his hair brush against my face for a moment. It was surprisingly soft, like a kitten's fur.

"Clark didn't say how beautiful you are," he said.

I scrunched my face at him.

Grant's eyebrows went up.

"What does that mean? You don't see it?"

"I'm so not."

He moved closer. His breath smelled like cinnamon.

"My nose is fat." Why would I tell him that? Maybe I was trying to push him away and draw him closer with the words. "Not to mention . . ." I patted my butt.

"Both perfect."

The lights in the room flickered on and off for a second,

though I wasn't sure if I had imagined it or not. The electric flicker in my body was proof enough. This wasn't Clark.

BEFORE GRANT LEFT, WE stood by the front door and he whispered in my ear, "Don't tell him, don't tell Clark. I just wanted to help but he'll be pissed."

"I'll try not to," I said.

"Don't try, Julie. Just don't do it. Trust me. I'll see you soon, okay?"

I nodded but it was hard for me to speak. My lips were tingling with electricity.

AFTER GRANT LEFT, I had a dream. I woke crouched on the floor and there were tears on my cheeks and my heart was knocking like it was trying to escape a death trap. In my dream, I had seen a car, a speeding car. Winding roads. A cliff. I was tumbling down, down, down, crashing against the rocks, flipping and hurtling and falling forever into the darkness and I knew that if I didn't wake up, everyone I loved would be gone forever.

THE NEXT DAY AT PE, I was walking past the basketball courts in the gym with the Olympic-sized pool under its floor when I saw a tall boy shooting hoops by himself. He made every shot.

My pulse dribbled along with the thud of the ball. Was

it Grant? At school? It couldn't be Clark. He never played basketball. As he had said, he couldn't even make a basket in a trash can. And this guy was good. I ran over, propelled by a blast of adrenaline, forgetting about trying to act cool.

"Hey!"

The boy, distracted, turned his head and missed the shot. He retrieved the basketball and stood looking at me, eyes out of focus, holding the ball to his chest like someone had extricated and handed him his own heart.

"Julie?"

"Clark?" I said. "What are you doing?"

He looked down at the ball and then rubbed his head. "I don't know."

"I didn't know you played."

"I don't."

"WHAT WAS THAT ABOUT?" I asked him on the way to lunch.

"I seriously don't know. I hate playing basketball." He pulled a knit cap with two pom-poms out of his pocket and jammed it on his head.

"You're good."

"No, I suck."

He was already agitated, so we didn't talk about the basketball playing anymore, and I didn't tell him about Grant. I wanted to say something; I felt as if I was being dishonest.

But what could I say? You deserted me and your hot twin brother came over last night and he kissed me? He told me not to tell you?

Why had I let Grant stay and talk? I didn't even know him. Maybe the resemblance to Clark had made him seem more familiar but it was still strange. He'd had an effect on me I didn't understand and I was pretty sure Clark wouldn't either.

Also I was still a little pissed at Clark. Not only because he had left so suddenly, when my grandmother was almost within reach. But why hadn't he told me about Grant in the first place? I had known him since the first day of school, seen him almost every day; I thought we trusted each other.

At lunch he had a pot of millet almond *kicharee* with yam and he offered me some; it was delicious, sweeter and creamier than his other recipe. I felt awkward, suddenly, being that close to him, after what had happened the night before. Clark and Grant were so alike that it was hard not to think about the spiced-candy scent of Grant's mouth as I watched Clark precisely chewing each bite of his food.

Jason Weitzman flicked the side of Clark's head as he passed by. "Nice pom-poms." For some reason he thought this was hysterically funny.

Clark frowned, rubbing his scalp. "What's wrong with pom-poms?"

"He's an ass. And pom-poms seem to have a negative effect on high school students who need to find something to hate on, apparently," I said.

"Not everyone is a hater." Clark waved at Ally Kellogg, who happened to be passing by.

"Does my hat annoy you?" he asked her.

She smiled with even teeth. The freckles across the bridge of her nose looked like someone had drawn them on in exactly the right place. "Not really. It kind of suits you."

"See?" Clark grinned at me. At least he was grinning again.

"I'm having a party this weekend," she said. "It's post-Halloween because we can't waste all the good decorations. Come in costume if you want. You should have enough hats to choose from." She handed us a flyer.

It was the first time I'd been invited to a party since I'd come to this school in September and Ally was super popular, one of the north-of-Wilshire rich kids who didn't socialize with south-of-Wilshires like me and Clark, so I was kind of flattered. She had complimented me on a short story I'd written about my grandmother in English, but besides that we hadn't talked much, in spite of our elementary school connection.

I thanked her and examined the invitation. "We should go," I told Clark.

"I'm not really into parties. Plus, it's kind of far to walk."

"You drive, though, right?" I knew he was eighteen, but we'd only ever gone places that were within walking distance.

He shrugged and shouldered his backpack. "I'm just not a party kind of guy," he said, turning away.

"Where are you going?"

"I have to pee. Is that okay with you?" There was a tiny edge to his voice, and for a second I wondered if he knew that Grant had visited me or if he was just still upset about the Ouija board incident.

"Are you mad?"

"Should I be?"

"No. Of course not. Sorry."

"See you later," said Clark, and I watched him lope away—long legs, wide, bony shoulders, dumb hat, backpack full of always-warm *kicharee*. I wondered again why I assumed Clark would mind that his brother and I had sat together on my bed. Maybe I was concerned about it. But not enough to stop hoping that Grant would come to see me again as he had promised.

I WAS FEELING THE desire for a little more of a social life than eating *kicharee* with Clark; I needed a bigger distraction from what was happening at my apartment—late-night visits from Luke and a crazy mom who still didn't have a job and the weirdness with Grant and the ever-present missing of my grandmother that nothing—not a friend, not a mysterious brother, not a stubborn Ouija board—could distract me from. So I decided to go to the party alone.

"Where are you off to?" my mom asked from my bedroom doorway while I was getting ready. "You look good."

I pushed a pair of my grandmother's marcasite hoops—dark, silvery metal flecked with shiny inlays—into the holes in my earlobes with a little more force than I had intended. "I got invited to Ally Kellogg's Halloween party. Remember the girl I know from fifth grade?"

My mom stood behind me so we were both reflected in the mirror on my wall. I was wearing a black off-the-shoulder jersey blouse and black high-heeled leather boots and a black-and-purple sequin-covered 1950s circle skirt that made my waist look small and hid my butt. I'd purchased it at Treasure Hunt, using most of my first paycheck. It was pretty clear by the creases on my mom's forehead and the way she touched her scraggly ponytail, her eyes darting back and forth between us in the mirror, that she didn't like how she looked, and it made me feel a twinge of guilt that I had been admiring myself when she came in. But it seemed like she only dressed up when Luke was around and didn't have the energy to do it otherwise. I wasn't sure what was worse—hooker heels or Mom the hot mess in a stained T-shirt and stretched-out yoga pants.

"I'm glad to see you getting out." She smiled wanly and pulled the ponytail holder out of her hair. I knew she meant what she said but, also, that part of her wanted me to stay. She didn't like to be alone and Luke had an out-of-town gig that night. They were seeing each other less. She was sleeping more again, had stopped preparing meals for us.

I adjusted a purple paisley silk scarf over my head and imagined Grant standing behind me instead of my mom, complimenting me the way he had the other night. Why did I care so much about someone I didn't know? I guess I was dressing for a guy, too, even though he wasn't there. I wondered if he might show up at the party and then scolded myself for wanting him to.

For some reason the thought of Grant made me remember the Ouija board in my closet. It would make a good accessory for my outfit. I went back into my room to get the board but hid it in the silk shawl I was wearing so my mom wouldn't see it.

"Do you need a ride?" she asked.

"No thanks." As I kissed her quickly on the cheek, I smelled her familiar, soapy scent and felt bad that I'd been so judgmental. "Clark is taking me."

Actually, I used the rest of my paycheck from Treasure

Hunt to take a cab to the party. I texted Clark on the way to see if he had changed his mind about coming, but he didn't answer.

Ally's house was a huge Tudor, decorated in hundreds of black and orange lights and nearly as many elaborately carved pumpkins. Life-sized mechanical skeletons danced in a circle on the vast lawn. Small plastic skulls, headless skeletons, and green cobwebs hung from the porch. Some of the sticky netting clung to my face and mouth, and even when I brushed it away, I could feel it against my chilled skin. My breath clouded the air like a little ghost escaping from my body. I could hear music coming from inside the house and saw costumed kids filing up the staircase.

The temperature soared as I walked inside. The music was too loud: Nirvana's "Smells Like Teen Spirit," a song I loved, but for some reason it made my mind hurt then. Colors blurred, shimmering in the hot air. Suddenly achingly hungry, I grabbed a handful of candy out of a crystal bowl on a counter. It made my gums ache but I took some more. I'd forgotten to eat dinner before I left. I was sure my grandma would never have allowed me to go to a Halloween party with an empty stomach, but my mom hadn't even asked me if I'd eaten.

Why had I come here at all? Ally, dressed as a sexy Alice in Wonderland in a blue pinafore and white thigh-high stockings, was running around the high-ceilinged, wall-papered rooms, handing people cups of punch.

"Hey."

"Hi, Ally."

"Want a drink?"

I took the plastic cup of rum punch from her gratefully.

"Are you a gypsy or something?"

"Yeah. Ouija board and all."

"Oh, cool! We'll set you up to answer people's questions," she said.

How could I say no to the hostess and the most popular girl at school? She sat me in a big red tapestry chair at a little gold table with lion's feet. I sipped my punch and my body started to relax and warm up a little, although my hands were still cold.

Jason Weitzman and Liam Wellington, two boys from my class both dressed as Jack Sparrow, approached my table.

"Hey, gypsy girl, I want my fortune told," Jason said.

He sat down opposite me.

"What do you want me to ask, Jack?"

"Uh, it's Jason."

"Yeah, I know. It was a joke. You know, Jack Sparrow," I said.

His lips curled under the fake mustache. "Ask it if Ally Kellogg is going to suck my dick."

I wanted to throw the board at him, but before I could do anything, the marker slid to NO. I couldn't help smirking a little.

Liam grabbed Jason in a headlock and scrubbed his scalp with his fist. "Poor baby."

Jason pushed him off, glaring at me. "Let's see how well you do, dude."

Elbowing Jason aside, Liam leaned over the table. He was too big, looming. I didn't like the feeling. "Tell me, fortune-teller, am I going to get laid tonight?"

The marker sped to NO. I could have told him that. I could have told them both.

"Fuck you," Liam said. He was laughing but it almost sounded like he was in pain. "I'm going to get laid, you sorry bitch."

The marker kept moving. I wanted to stop it, but my hands felt glued to the surface.

F-U-C-K-Y-O-U

"Bitch," Liam said again.

I got up, folded the Ouija board in my shawl, and started to walk away. At this point I really just wanted to get out of there.

I felt a hand on my ass and whirled around to face Jason and Liam. But I saw their faces blanch as someone behind me said, "Don't touch her."

Surprisingly neither Jason nor Liam said anything else. They just walked away.

"I was hoping you'd be here. That's the only reason I came," he said. The boy took off the top hat he wore and smoothed his hair back. His face was painted white with dark marks to look like a Day of the Dead skeleton.

"Clark?" I said, unsure.

There was a long pause.

"Grant," he said.

WTF? It was just wrong that I couldn't tell them apart.

"This is messed up." I walked away from him and he followed me. I had hoped to see Grant but now it just gave me the creeps and I wanted to go home. And I was still upset from what had happened with Jason and Liam.

"Red Right Hand" by Nick Cave and the Bad Seeds was playing. Katie Turnbull had a noose around her neck and was starting a conga line, followed by M. J. Rodgers with plastic fangs and white glitter on his skin, and two girls I didn't know in cat ears and tails and black spandex American Apparel unitards.

"Wait."

I went through the French doors and into the garden, and Grant was right behind me. The large stone statues had been wrapped in gauze like mummies. Neon-green cobwebs draped the bushes. A Frankenstein statue repeatedly raised and lowered a giant ax, and a mechanical witch cackled as she offered up a dead baby doll on a plate. Except for the bloodred water, the tiled pool reminded me of a much larger version of our old one. I thought that if I still lived in that house, if my grandmother hadn't died, I wouldn't be at this stupid party dogged by whichever the hell brother I was with.

He was handing me a cup of punch. Which I reluctantly took. Molly Neiman, dressed as the Bride of Frankenstein, ran by screaming, pulling her shirt over her beehive hairdo. Grant didn't even glance at her boobs.

"I was worried about the other night. That I upset you," he said.

"I feel weird not telling Clark." I missed Clark then with a hollow pang that surprised me. All his oddness seemed like the only normal thing in my life just then and I wanted to get home and call him. "He's my friend."

"I know." Grant stepped closer.

I stepped back. "I thought you were him. Where is he? I texted him and he didn't answer."

"Home. You know how he is. Everything freaks him out."

I squinted at him, trying to figure out if he was being disrespectful to Clark or just teasing in an affectionate way. And if it was the former, should I defend my friend?

"Did you borrow his hat?"

Grant looked at the hat in his hand. "Oh, yes, this. It's not really my thing. But it's Halloween. You know, costumes?"

I shook my head in confusion, looking away at the haunted garden and bloody pool. Suddenly colors seemed much too bright and the mechanical witch's cackle reverberated through my head. A glowing blue devil with horns uncannily sprouting from her forehead whacked me with her tail as she passed. My clothes felt tight. Grant was watching me. "I need to get home," I said.

"Can I give you a ride?"

I went back into the house and was immediately sheathed in sweat. "Mind Eraser" clanged wickedly against my eardrums as I passed Harry Potter (Devin Li) and Hermione (Emily Carr) making out on the staircase, and headed toward the front door. Grant followed me, pushing a Jack Sparrow out of the way. On the porch, the headless plastic skeletons tried to ensnare me in their long fingers. I noticed one of the pumpkins had begun to rot, caving in on itself, the way my heart sometimes felt in my chest since my grandma died. The smell of the pumpkin reminded me for a second of the funeral parlor where we had received her ashes. For the first time, I realized she had actually been taken apart there, burned, put in a jar. Ally's house loomed, white and wailing as a ghost.

"Please," Grant said, his voice floating across the night like mist. "I'll take you home."

I stood on the sidewalk, dialing the cab. He hovered behind me, as tall as Clark, but his presence was so much more imposing. I felt his hand on my arm.

"Come on, I have a car. You'll save cab fare. I'll just drop you off."

"This is so weird. You need to stop dressing like him and just showing up."

He tipped the topper at me. "What, only one of us can wear hats all of a sudden?" I thought of how Clark had worn the same hat but not as a costume. I missed him but he hadn't come with me; he hadn't even texted me back. Grant was here, offering me a ride. He'd defended me against Jason and Liam while Clark hid at home.

I followed Grant down the driveway to the street where his mom's Volvo station wagon was parked; he hadn't valeted.

He opened the door for me gallantly and I slid inside, breathing with relief at being away from the stifling heat and ear-slamming sounds of the party. There was a Virgin Mary on the dashboard. I touched her with one finger.

"My mom's scared of accidents," Grant said. "Terrified. So's the Clark man."

"Does this help?"

"Here's hoping."

I looked at his profile. It was uncanny, the resemblance.

"I always wondered about twins," I said. "I bet you never feel alone."

He shrugged. "You'd be surprised."

"So, you're not that close?" I took off the silk scarf around my head. It was damp and sheer with sweat.

"Oh, yeah, we're really close. It's complicated. What about you? Who are you close to?"

I stared out the car window at the lights shimmering behind a gauzy layer of fog. "I was close to my mom but not so much anymore. And my grandma."

"Yeah. Clark mentioned that. I'm sorry. You were trying to reach her with the Ouija board?"

I nodded, still not looking at him, and squeaked my finger down the cold glass.

"Do you think those things work?" Grant asked.

I shrugged. "I have no idea."

"Maybe I can help you."

We pulled up in front of my apartment and I saw Luke's truck parked there. So much for the out-of-town gig. One female in the house would be happy.

Grant studied my face. "Are you all right?"

"My mom's boyfriend is over. He kind of creeps me out."

"I'm sorry." He leaned closer. His fingers brushed my

cheek with the back of his hand but so lightly I could hardly feel it, as if he'd touched me with a thought. Warmth filled me, and my muscles relaxed for the first time all night. There was something so familiar about him; maybe it was just because of how much he looked like Clark. I didn't feel as shy as I would have expected.

"You don't wear it down much."

I had no idea what he was talking about.

"Your hair. It's pretty."

I mumbled a thank-you.

"Would you like me to come in? Maybe we can try the Ouija board thing again."

"Yeah, actually. I'd like you there." I hadn't expected to say that. But I didn't feel like facing Luke and his canned beans alone.

Grant glided from the car and came around to help me out. I walked up the stairs in front of him, aware of his eyes on my hips in the gypsy skirt. When we got inside, I saw a light on in the kitchen and heard heavy metal playing. Shit.

Luke looked up from the stove, primly tucking his hair behind his ears. His bare chest was pale and slightly concave and he wore a pair of black fishnets under black knee-length bondage pants, and eyeliner. To keep from screaming about his attire, I had to remind myself it was a few days after Halloween and that he was in a band.

Grant, who had paused in the living room, came in behind me. Luke, startled, glared at him and his jaw jerked.

"Who's this?" he asked. He hadn't met Clark yet so I didn't have to explain that, at least.

Grant held out his hand. "I'm Grant, sir."

I was impressed. Luke didn't look like a sir, most especially not in fishnets.

He didn't shake. "It's late," he said. His voice reminded me of the sharp kitchen knife he'd brought over to cut the crust off his sandwiches. He thought our knives were too dull. His eyes, staring at Grant, cut more sharply.

I took Grant's hand, more in defiance of Luke than anything, and led him to my room. Luke called after us but I ignored him. He wasn't my parent; he couldn't tell me what to do.

Grant stood in the doorway, looking like he wasn't sure if he should cross the threshold, but I gestured to the bed. He came over and we sat side by side, not touching but so close I could feel waves of warmth coming off him, comforting on this cold night. I was glad I'd let him drive me home and come inside.

When I set the Ouija board down, he picked it up and examined it. "This innocent-looking little item could have gotten us both into trouble."

"Thanks for stepping in," I said.

"Where'd you get it?"

"I found it in a drawer in the apartment when we moved here. One night I just missed my grandma so much. . . ."

"I'm sorry." He turned to face me and there was no sign of teasing in his eyes.

"Thanks."

"You were really close to her."

"Yes." I swallowed, uncomfortable under his gaze. "My life changed so fast after she died. We lost our house, my mom went nuts, started dating this random guy." Why was I telling him so much so quickly? Just because he looked like Clark?

"Yeah, you don't know who you're going to meet online." He nodded toward the kitchen. "What was that all about?"

"Weird. I told you."

"I guess so. What's his problem?"

"I have no idea," I said. "But he looked at you like he'd seen a ghost or something."

Grant put down the Ouija board and moved closer, leaning back on one arm, slightly behind me on the mattress. "I'm no ghost," he said. There was a tone to his voice that I couldn't quite put my finger on. Sad? Determined? But also pained.

I looked back and into his eyes (with him leaning back we were at equal eye level), challenging. Why did I say what I said next? It was so unlike me to flirt that overtly—to flirt at all. "Prove that you're not a ghost," I said.

"You asked for it."

Since I had never been kissed before, I didn't have much to compare it to. But it seemed to me from what I had read about kissing and seen on TV and in movies that it didn't normally make you feel as if you were levitating. When Grant kissed me, the lights went on and off and it seemed my body lifted gently off the bed and into the ether, completely weightless, stars flickering on around us and the world far below, turning, blue and green and brown, so precious, the most perfect, vulnerable thing you have ever seen.

AFTER THAT KISS, WHICH was not just any kiss, I felt I owed it to Clark to let him know. *Not that he'll care,* I told myself. *Not that I have led him on, ever.* But it made me uneasy that I hadn't mentioned Grant to him yet. When Grant left— I'd been firm, even though part of me wanted him to stay longer—he had asked me again not to tell Clark, and I had asked why, when he said that Clark had a crush on me.

"I don't want to hurt him anymore," Grant had said. I didn't necessarily believe Clark liked me that way, but I thought if he did, that was all the more reason to bring it up. I didn't let Grant know. I pretended to agree.

At school Clark and I had been able to stay under the radar, miraculously, in spite of his hats and smiling habit, but after Ally's Halloween party we weren't that lucky.

Jason Weitzman and Liam Wellington approached us at lunch on Monday. I guess they had spent the rest of their weekend hatching a sophisticated plan to get back at me and Grant, whom they probably thought was Clark, for what had happened at the party.

"Hey, gypsy, how's that Ouija board working out for you?" Jason said.

I turned away, trying to ignore them.

"Because Liam and I weren't too happy about how it spoke to us. And we just wanted you to know that we have our eyes on your ass."

"And that's not too hard to do," Liam said, making a wide gesture with his hands on either side of his hips.

"Hey," Clark said. "Stop." They imitated him in high voices and walked off, laughing. It was amazing to see how differently they had reacted to Grant in spite of his identical appearance. I found myself wishing for Grant again, but I had wished for Clark at the party before Grant got there. Maybe what I really wanted was both of them? At least Jason and Liam hadn't mentioned seeing Clark at Ally's, forcing me to tell him that I'd met his brother.

"Seriously?" I said, tugging at his red-green-and-yellow beanie to try to take my mind off the whole thing. "Are you Rasta now or something?"

"I like the colors." He paused, examining me as if for bruises. "Did something happen at the party?"

"I brought the Ouija board, and they asked me dumb-ass questions and didn't like the answers. It's nothing."

"Are you okay?"

"Sure," I said. "I'm fine. They're just assholes. What do you expect? We're in high school."

"Thank God not for much longer. Can I still come over after school?"

I took a shriveled apple from my lunch box and noticed he wasn't eating. "What, no *kicharee*?"

He shrugged. "I haven't been feeling like cooking much lately."

SO WHEN WE GOT home, I found some old fortune cookies my mom had brought back from a date with Luke, and made some tea. The cookies were stale and salty. Clark's fortune said, A VISITOR FROM YOUR PAST HAS ARRIVED. Mine said, USE DELICACY WHEN HANDLING FRAGILE THINGS.

I looked at my friend. He didn't appear fragile, although his bones were as thin as they were long, and there was an earnestness in his eyes that made him seem susceptible to bullying.

Maybe I shouldn't say anything? Maybe Grant was right?

"Let's practice our report." Clark stood up. He pointed at me. "Did you know that car crashes are the leading cause of death for teenagers in the United States? Teen drivers between the ages of sixteen and nineteen are four times more likely to crash. Add alcohol into the mix and the results are even more deadly." He took a piece of black cloth out of his backpack and put it over his head so only his eyes showed through the slits. It was an executioner's hood.

"What the hell is that?" I asked.

"A prop. For our report. I'm the Grim Reaper."

"You're scaring me. Take it off."

He cackled from under the folds of material.

"Seriously!" I said. I was starting to sweat through the armpits of my vintage silk blouse, and the room felt too small.

He took the hood off and sat down next to me. "Did that really scare you?" he asked in his soft voice, the one he saved for moments like this, when we weren't teasing each other anymore.

"Yes."

"Sorry. I was trying to add some drama." He threw the hood onto the floor. "It was a bad idea."

I picked it up. "No. I've just been more sensitive lately about stuff like that."

He nodded.

"And it seems like something this serious . . . I don't want them to laugh."

"I thought you liked how my hats make you laugh."

"Not this one. It's not funny."

"I know," he said, "believe me, dude, I know," and his face was suddenly pale, blood drained; he did look fragile, ready to crumble, like the fortune cookie said. He took the hood from my hand, balled it up in his backpack with a grimace. "I don't even know why I brought that thing at all. It's like someone else made me bring it or something." He chewed on his cuticle.

"What do you mean, someone else?"

"I don't know. I was at Target with my mom the other day and I saw it with the sale Halloween costumes and I bought it, even though it's so not my thing. And then when I was coming over here, I guess I grabbed it, but I don't really remember."

I frowned at him. "You don't remember?"

"I have these sort of blackout things lately. I can't really explain. It started on Halloween just after I left your house."

The window was open; a breeze came in and shivered my shoulders. I wrapped a blanket around myself. "What kind of blackouts? That sounds serious."

"Not really blackouts. Just, I get disoriented and I forget stuff. It's nothing, Julie. I just, I don't know, I just think I'm kind of stressed lately."

I wondered if he would tell me about his estranged brother; it was the perfect time. But instead he said, "Hey, I've got to leave. My mom wants me home early tonight."

So neither of us had brought up Grant, again; I didn't care to admit to myself that I might not want to tell Clark because of what his brother had already given to me that he could not.

BUT IT DID COME up two nights later when Clark was over again. And Luke arrived, earlier than usual. It was always disconcerting to see him before ten. Actually it was always disconcerting to see him at all. Clark and I were cramming to finish our report, eating some of my mom's chocolate-bar stash in the kitchen to help us power through, when Luke walked in. His feet were bare and the way he stuck out his belly and turned in his feet reminded me of a scary-looking toddler learning to walk.

"Hello, Julie."

Just before Luke spoke, I realized that I had to get Clark out of there. But it was too late.

"Grant," Luke said.

Clark turned. He was holding the candy bowl and it fell out of his hands and broke on the floor. I looked down at the shards near Luke's bare feet. There were some flecks of blood on the pale skin.

"Damn." Luke grimaced at me as he reached to grab his foot. "Get that cleaned up, would you?" He dabbed at the blood with a paper towel, swearing under his breath, then threw the towel in the trash and hobbled out.

"What did he say?"

"Get that cleaned up?" I offered, trying to avoid the whole thing.

"He said 'Grant.'" Clark spoke in a monotone. I was kneeling on the floor sweeping up pieces of the bowl, trying to hide my reddening face. "He said 'Grant.' How does he know about Grant?"

There was a word flashing in my head over and over in neon red: *Danger.*

"Clark, I met your brother."

"You what?" I saw the tendons in his neck strain. And I hadn't even said anything about the kiss yet.

"Julie," Clark said slowly, in a way I had never heard him enunciate my name. "My brother, Grant, was in a car accident a year ago. He's dead."

PART II

Who influences Flowers

THE GHOST

1

Maybe my friend was crazy, psychotic crazy, pretending that his brother was dead or pretending that he was his dead brother. Or maybe there was another explanation, and it didn't make me feel too relieved either.

He was in a car accident, Clark had said. A year ago.

I took him by the wrist and dragged him, stumbling, into my room, where he sat on the floor with his knees drawn up under his chin and his head down, his face hidden under his baseball cap, and I told him everything that had happened. I could tell he didn't want me to see him cry, but of course he was crying, who wouldn't?

"How could it be?" he kept saying. "It can't . . ."

Outside, the Santa Anas thrashed the trees against the window like a giant poltergeist at work. I stared into the darkness for a long time, listening to our breath. Then I turned back to Clark.

His shadow loomed behind him on the wall, making him look like a small boy in contrast. But something was wrong; the shadow didn't match.

It wasn't wearing the baseball cap, as if it weren't Clark's shadow at all. A trick of the light. Clark stood up and the shadow stretched, blending into the darkness.

"Sit down," I said softly, patting the mattress next to me. "Sit down, Clark."

He was pacing and pulling at his hair so that it stood out in little tufts around his face. "I have to leave."

"Don't leave, please. We'll figure this out together."

"Figure what out? That I'm psycho boy? What do they call it? Multiple personality? Schizophrenia? I thought I just had a mood disorder." He was speaking too loudly, and I was afraid Luke would hear.

"You're not crazy."

"Then what? Grant came back from the dead and took over my body without me knowing? That makes me feel a whole hell of a lot better." He slumped down beside me and began massaging his temples.

"Remember when I asked you if you believed in ghosts? You didn't really say. Do you know much about them?"

"No, I just always felt like it was possible. After he died,

I got this feeling that he wasn't entirely gone." He looked up at me and there was so much pain in his eyes that it jabbed into my stomach.

I grabbed him and pulled him close before he could push me away. But he didn't push me away. I knew his body better now. I had hugged and kissed it, perhaps animated by a different soul, but his. He was shaking so much, I thought it was me.

And I could easily be shaking; I had maybe just met, had kissed, my first ghost, in the body of my best friend. I was no stranger to supernatural content in books, TV, and film, but it was one thing to try to reach my grandmother through a Ouija board and quite another to meet a real ghost who could take over a flesh-and-blood body. Clark was right; it was insane, it was too freakin' much.

He was blushing, and I wondered if it had been wrong of me to hug him like that. *After you kissed his brother. His dead brother.* I let go and put my hands in my lap like they were foreign objects.

"Listen," he said after a moment, in a deeper voice. He sat up straight again and he wasn't blushing. His face looked pale and still. "I missed you," he said.

As if I'd just stared directly into a bright light, red streaks of veins patterned the insides of my eyelids. In my head there was a sound like someone screaming in the middle of the night when you're not sure if you're hearing a party or a murder. And I wanted to scream and run the hell out of there, but instead I smoothed my homemade map-of-California tablecloth skirt over my knees, shifted away from him, and said quietly, "Grant?"

He didn't move, just stood staring like he was trying to hypnotize me, which perhaps he had already done before. Why else had I kissed him so readily, without even knowing him at all? His eyes reminded me of the far-seeing gaze of my ancestors in the disintegrating velvet photo album. I remembered the levitation sensation when he kissed me, the world spinning away below us. I wondered if this was like sleepwalking, if I could wake Clark without scaring the shit out of him.

"What are you feeling now? What's this about?" I asked in my best imitation of the therapist I had seen as a kid. But he hadn't been very helpful and neither was I.

Grant shook his head. "It's not like that."

"Then what is it like, Grant? Please try to explain it to me. Could it be that Clark missed you so much that he started thinking he was you?" I was still trying some amateur psychology without knowing what the hell I was doing.

"I miss him too," Grant said. His voice was low and his eyes downcast.

"I still don't understand."

"When you used the board thing. I came back. Somehow.

There was something about the two of you using it together that made it work."

My skin crawled on my bones like it belonged to someone else.

"The Ouija board?"

"Yeah, whatever it's called. I thought those were just kids' toys, but I guess not."

G-R-A-N. I remembered what the board had spelled. I had thought it was going to spell *grandma*. But maybe Clark had made it spell Grant because he subconsciously wanted his brother to come back? Or maybe his brother really did?

I felt as if I was a plastic doll whose limbs were being arranged by a devious child. I needed some time and space to think.

I went to the door and opened it, pointing. "I need you to leave now," I told him in a way I would never speak to Clark.

"Julie," he said. "You're sure about that? I don't entirely understand this either, but I think I can help you. With your grandmother. There are a lot of things I know."

"Get out," I said, though I wondered what he knew. If he was really a ghost—not that I believed it, but if—he would know about death. Maybe he knew how I could reach my grandma.

I heard him, whoever he was, go out the front door and

when I looked through the window, I saw him running down the street, so fast and sure-footed, not like Clark at all. The streetlights shone red, reflected in a puddle of dirty water.

I pressed my forehead against the cool, water-spotted glass, wishing I knew what to do. I obviously couldn't ask Clark. My mom was in Lukeland. My grandmother, the one I needed most, was the most gone of all.

So I went to my computer and sat down at the screen. I didn't want to know the answer, but there really wasn't a choice.

GRANT, I typed in. MORRISON. CHICAGO, ILLINOIS.

And there he was:

Grant Morrison, seventeen, an honor student and star player on the Hancock Bulldogs basketball team, was killed in a hit-and-run incident this Saturday, January 2. He died on the scene at 12:03 a.m. Police are still searching for a 1999 red Honda Accord. Grant is survived by his parents, Lisa and Hal Morrison, and his twin brother, Clark Morrison. Funeral services will be held this coming Sunday.

Now I was levitating again, but for a different reason. Leaving my body with fear. I had dreamed about Grant's death in a car crash the night I had met him. I wasn't only afraid of ghosts now. I was afraid of myself.

AT DAWN I WOKE, after a night of restless sleep, and tiptoed to my mom's door. It was open and when I looked into her bedroom I saw that Luke wasn't there—thank God. He usually left really early in the morning.

"Mom?" I whispered, stepping into the room.

She stirred and I put my hand on her back. Her body felt warm and soft with sleep. I wished she could hold me like I was a baby.

"Sweetie?" She reached out and took my hand. "Did you have a dream?"

"I need to talk to you," I said. I wanted to tell her everything. The colors, the sounds, the Ouija board, trying to reach my grandmother, what was happening to Clark. And especially about Grant.

She sat up and put on the light. "Oh, baby. I haven't been sleeping well. Can we talk later?"

"Never mind." I backed away, afraid that in my stressed state I would say something really harsh about her dating disgusting men.

"You know you can always talk to me."

"No, I can't. You're always either sleeping or with Luke or both." It was the kindest I could manage.

"And you have Clark now," she said. *Touché.*

"I don't have Clark. He's not my boyfriend or anything. I told you!"

"But he's a good friend to you, right? I like him." She moved to the side and opened her arms so I could climb into bed with her the way I used to, before Luke came. "Come here. Let's just rest awhile." I was tempted. But when I got too close, it smelled nauseatingly like him. My skin suddenly itched.

"I'm going to shower," I said. "It's almost morning."

But it didn't feel that way. It felt darker than ever.

I KNEW I HAD to talk to someone. For a moment I considered Ms. Merritt, but I couldn't let her think I was crazy. She was the only person besides Clark who seemed to care about my college applications.

I wanted to talk to Clark, the real Clark. Even if it upset him, I felt he had to know.

I was so relieved when I saw him at school the next day, wearing a fez. Part of me thought he wouldn't come or that he would come as the wrong brother, but the hat reassured me. What I didn't know was if he would be angry with me for everything that had happened. He might not know about the kiss, even though his body had participated, but he knew that I'd hidden my meetings with Grant from him.

I walked up tentatively. "Nice fez."

"Hi." He had dark half-circles under his eyes.

"I need to talk to you," I said. We went and sat on our bench. I picked a dead leaf from one of the large potted plants and crushed it in my hand; it made a crackling sound. "How do you feel? What do you remember about last night?"

He shrugged. "I remember talking to you about my brother and then just blanking out, and when I woke up, it was morning, but I felt like I hadn't slept at all." He squinted up at me. "Do you think I'm schizophrenic?"

I started to touch him and then pulled my hand away, wondering if that might trigger Grant, although it didn't seem like Grant would want to show up at boring high school. Except for a brief basketball game, it seemed he preferred parties and girls' bedrooms. Or maybe the touch would just trigger me. Touching Clark was so different from touching his brother, but in fact it might be exactly the same, and yet not. My head thumped with the thoughts. "I don't think so. But the alternative isn't really comforting."

He looked at me narrowly. "What's the alternative?"

I didn't want to tell him that Grant had come back and explained about the possession, but I had to let him know that it was a possibility, however far-fetched. "That Grant took over your body in some way. That his spirit came through when we used the Ouija board."

I tensed for his reaction, but he only looked up at me sadly. What must it have been like to grow up with a twin, someone who had formed into a person beside you in the same womb, walked at your side for seventeen years, looked exactly like you? Someone who was stronger, faster, better at sports, more confident than you were. Someone you wanted to be and resented all at the same time. And then they were gone and you wished you had never felt anything except gratitude to have your double, your second heart.

"If it's true, what should we do about it?" he asked me.

"What people do in books and on TV when this type of shit happens."

He waited.

"Think *Buffy*," I said.

"Research."

WE WENT TO CLARK's house because I didn't feel like seeing my mom. Clark had said his parents weren't too into him having company, which is why we hadn't gone there before, but he thought it would be okay under the circumstances.

He lived in one of the small stucco houses south of Wilshire, some carefully tended roses lining the front path, a neat green lawn. A basketball net hung on the garage door, and I thought of Clark saying he sucked at basketball, and of the article about Grant. *Star player.* No wonder Clark said he hated the sport.

Inside, the light was dim and it smelled stuffy, as if the windows weren't opened often. I wondered if there were pictures of Grant on the mantelpiece, but we went straight upstairs to Clark's bedroom. No pictures of his brother there. The room was very sparsely furnished and the walls were bare. His books and hats were scattered around. I wondered why he hadn't brought more with him when he moved from Chicago. Maybe it was another way to forget.

I sat next to him on the bed, but not too close, and I showed him an occult website I had Googled the night before.

"'Spirits can become activated and released by Ouija boards and enter through a portal,'" Clark read in a whisper from the screen. "'They are especially likely to come when the board is handled by psychics or sensitives. Spirits to whom a living person has a strong attachment are more likely to come through, as are those with unfinished business.'" He glanced up at me, then looked quickly away and continued reading. "'In some cases, malevolent spirits will attach themselves to others, coming through relatively unnoticed. All spirits may manifest through household appliances, creating shaking, bumping, hammering, and other auditory disturbances. Some of these behaviors are capricious, others much more dangerous. Both evil and well-meaning spirits may also attach themselves to the body of a vulnerable human 'host.' This is otherwise known as possession.'"

I shivered so that even my hair follicles tingled, cold. Clark's face looked paler than usual and his Adam's apple more prominent. Behind him, I noticed, plugged in beside his bed, a small night-light. We weren't kids anymore, but we both still needed reassurance in the dark.

"This is so fucked up, either way," he said. "What am I supposed to do?"

"What do you want to do?"

"Get him the hell out of my head!" Clark muttered, but when he looked up at me his eyes were bigger and softer than I had ever seen them and I thought he might cry again.

He pulled off his hat and leaned forward so his elbows were on his knees, his head down. "Everyone loved him. It was so weird because we looked so much alike, but that had nothing to do with it."

I nodded, trying to think of something to say, but I couldn't imagine what the right words would be.

"We were so close but we were different. He was good at everything—sports, school, people; everyone was crazy about him. I get good grades but I have to work. Everything was easy for him. If I'm honest, there were times I wished he wasn't, we weren't . . ."

He winced when he said this and I found myself wincing, too.

"But I never wanted him dead!" Clark turned to me and I could see the tension rising in his body. I was almost afraid he'd run away again, like he did when we'd used the Ouija board—run off down the street and leave me alone in his bedroom.

"I know," I said. I reached out and touched the back of his hand where the veins looked thick with blood. "Of course not, Clark."

"What about you?" he said, and although his tone was mostly sad, there was an accusation hidden way down beneath that. "Do you want to get rid of him?"

"Clark . . ."

"Never mind." He stood up. "Forget it. What the hell am I saying? Get rid of him? I sound insane. Like I believe I could get rid of a . . . someone who isn't even alive."

There was a pause and I heard a car alarm scream outside. And then, in a deeper voice, my friend said, "Yeah. That sounds pretty insane."

I looked up and I knew it was Grant sitting there. But the weird thing was, I didn't want to run.

He pressed his forehead to mine and I closed my eyes; there was so much heat where we touched and a red color shining behind my eyelids. His long fingers wrapped my wrist with room to spare and he lifted my arm that way and then flattened his palm against mine. His palms were calloused and warm, and his hands made mine look tiny.

"Look at me," he said.

I glanced up for a second, then down again.

"Is it hard for you to look at me?" His voice was so different from Clark's. Either this was real or Clark was a gifted actor who should have applied to the Actors Studio instead of MIT.

"I don't know who you are."

"Do you know who you are?"

I had no idea what he meant. It was like he was the one practicing psychology on me now.

"If you really know who you are, then it doesn't matter as much who I am. You will know you can trust me if you trust yourself."

What kind of line was that? A pretty good one; it made my brain feel like a kaleidoscope he was playing with.

"You're not Clark," I said.

He nodded and I made myself look into his eyes. They were Clark's eyes, but Grant hovered behind them, and I realized how much I wanted both brothers in that moment.

"It sucks being dead," he said matter-of-factly.

"I would imagine." I didn't want to be sarcastic but I wasn't sure how to respond. To take the edge off, I asked him what it was like. If this was for real (and I guess I was at least partially hoping it was real), I wanted to know. I wanted to understand what my grandmother had felt.

"It's cold. Not like what you call cold. Maybe like hospital-metal, morgue, frozen-meat cold. Obviously you never get to do shit. I was going to be an emergency room doctor. How ironic, right? You never get to fall in love. And it's weird, watching you all walk around, acting as if it's never going to happen to any of you; even if you've lost someone, you act like it won't ever happen to you and you take all the things you get to do for granted. It's weird for me because there's this person who looks just like me, who has my same genetics, walking around and alive. And getting to be with you." He seemed to come out of a brief trance and stared at me as if he could see through my skin. "Why?"

"Why what?"

"Why do you want to know about it? Your grand-mother?"

I nodded. That was all I could manage without tears.

He moved even closer. I could swear he smelled different from Clark. How could that be? "You really want to com-municate with her, right?"

I didn't say a word, didn't even nod this time, as if I could protect myself this way.

"I can help you," he told me. "If you let me."

"How can you help me?"

Grant tapped his knuckles against his palm. "You need

to go to your old house. Where her spirit is. She's not around here."

"How do you know?"

"I just do."

"Then how did you come back? The accident was in Illinois."

"Because of you." He leaned in and brushed my hair from my face. "I want to be close to you," he whispered. "And luckily Clark found you. But I don't have much time."

"What does that mean?"

"Never mind. I just mean I need you."

"Why me?" I pushed on his chest to make him look me in the eyes now. He smiled, his face so close I could count every eyelash, see the faint glimmer of sweat on his temples.

"You helped me come back," he said. "Without you I couldn't have come."

I tried to remember to breathe; my head was a carousel of spinning lights.

"You have a gift, to bring back the . . . you brought me back. I'm indebted to you. You understand."

"I don't understand anything. I wanted my grandmother, but I've lost my best friend."

"Lost him? You haven't lost Clark. You have us both now."

"He's losing his mind."

Grant shook his head. "No, he's not. This is real."

I wanted to push him away again. But the thing was, I was starting to believe him. "And I still don't know why you chose me."

"Without you I couldn't have come. You're powerful, Julie. You don't know it yet, but you are. Gifted. Alive and powerful."

"I am not," I said. "I can't even bring my grandmother back, even in a dream!"

"And beautiful," Grant said, ignoring me.

I shook my head and he grasped my shoulders in his hands and made me look at him. "Stop hiding." He moved a stray hair out of my eyes. "You're beautiful. My brother is in love with you."

I tensed as he put his lips lightly to mine, and then I pulled away. "That's not really a reason for me to let you kiss me," I said.

He paused, as if trying to hypnotize me with his eyes, and then leaned in again and this time I let him. And like before, the world rushed away, like going into outer space and watching the Earth from far, far off, stars exploding inside my body while the little planet got smaller and smaller. I felt, rather than heard, music I couldn't describe, vibrating in my solar plexus, making my rib cage shake. My mouth burned like spicy sugar candy. I gasped for breath.

When I heard the knock on the door, it took a moment to register.

Then a woman's voice said, "Clark?"

And the spells were all broken. He fell away, staring at me like I was a stranger. Grant was gone.

"Hang on, Mom." He jumped up and glared at me. Went to the door. "I have company." They talked some more, too softly for me to hear, and then he came back inside and locked the door behind him.

"What the hell is going on? What were we doing?"

"Kissing," I said. I couldn't look at him. But it was for a different reason than why I hadn't been able to look at Grant.

"Kissing? You were kissing him?"

I shook my head. "No. Yes. I was kissing you."

"I wasn't here."

It amazed me, still, how different he looked when Grant was gone. He seemed so much more agitated, awkward. Even his body appeared thinner, smaller. I held out my hand to him and he shook his head. "You were here at first. . . ."

He stared at the carpet, shaking his head. "You better go."

"Clark?"

"You better go," he said again.

I went through the back door, not wanting to face his mother or the photos that might be on the mantelpiece.

THERE WERE SO MANY things running around in my brain, little thoughts with feet and shoes. Some were on team Grant and some were on team Clark. They faced off like rabid tweens in their designated T-shirts at a *Twilight* premiere, making me sick.

"Clark is kind and already your best friend," said the practical girl self who wore a flowered cotton dress, denim jacket, and flat suede boots, who wouldn't shut up about her college applications and the fact that she got straight A's. "Take the best friend every time! You know what happy couples always say, 'I married my best friend. That's why it lasted.'"

"Grant is hot and tortured," said the similarly tortured romantic inner goth. "So what if he's dead? When he takes over Clark's body, he sure doesn't feel dead."

If I was honest with myself, I wanted them both. I wanted a best friend and I wanted someone who wasn't afraid of everything. Grant might have been dead (I was starting to believe that he was a spirit and not a psychosis), but he wasn't afraid; he *was* the darkness that drew me toward it. Clark was still a boy who couldn't face the dark.

My mom wasn't home when I got there—out with Luke, I figured. So I made myself a bowl of cornflakes and went to my room. I missed Clark's cooking, the warm, savory grains and the surprise flavors of herbs and seasonings. Bowls of adzuki beans, brown rice, and arame seaweed to ground us. I needed something to ground me. I needed someone to help.

My grandmother would have been able to listen and understand the situation. My mother, for all her supernatural storytelling, seemed too fragile to talk to, especially about something as strange as this. And she felt as gone as Grandma.

I got out the Ouija board and held it on my lap. The plastic stuck to my bare skin. It seemed I had brought someone back with the board, even if it wasn't my grandmother. I wondered if I could try again and get the right spirit this time.

But when I set my fingers on the marker, there was no movement at all. I wondered if Grant could help me, Grant with his knowledge of that cold, cold meat-locker world.

RIGHT BEFORE I FELL asleep, I put my grandmother's photo under my bed and asked again for her to come visit me in a dream, if not through the Ouija board.

As I slept, black-and-white images flickered behind my eyelids like a silent movie. I was searching for Grandma Miriam, walking through a series of rooms that looked like the backdrops in the ancestor photo album. The people in old-fashioned suits and dresses were seated on claw-foot chairs or wicker settees, or standing stiffly posed. They didn't move when I passed, only shifted their strange, pale eyes to follow me. Then I was in a fancy room, a kind of parlor with large mirrors on the walls. There were two tall boys, one wearing a bowler hat and both sitting upright, side by side, their eyes large and farseeing crystals.

"Whatever happens, leave the light on," said Clark.

"Turn off the lights," argued Grant without moving his mouth.

He stood up and the room fell away into a terrible darkness.

I WENT TO SCHOOL the next day, eager to see Clark and apologize again, but he wasn't there and he didn't text me back when I tried him. At home my mom was sleeping in her bedroom and there were no groceries in the fridge. I thought again about Clark's *kicharee,* how he always used to serve me a generous bowl, extolling the virtues of the kinds of seaweeds or spices he had used. What was wrong with me? Why had I even considered choosing his dead brother over him? There was no way I could have them both. I called but he didn't answer.

In the evening, my mom woke up and shuffled out of her bedroom in dingy slippers that resembled large dust bunnies.

"What's wrong?" I asked.

"Nothing."

"Don't lie to me. It messes with my intuition."

She sighed and sat at the table. There were crumbs on the gray kitchen linoleum and I thought of getting up to sweep them away, but didn't.

"What do you mean, messes with?"

"I can tell you're upset. I get these strong feelings and if you don't validate them, it makes me not trust myself."

She tugged her hair back into a ragged ponytail and her face looked thinner than usual. "Luke hasn't been calling. I think he's avoiding me."

"Maybe that's not such a bad thing," I said.

"What about you?" she asked. "How is Clark?"

"Not so great. We had a fight." I felt a bubble of tension expanding in my chest, ready to burst open with relief when I told her what was going on. But just then the phone rang.

"Oh, sorry, honey, I have to get this," she said, checking the caller ID. "It's Luke."

CLARK WASN'T AT SCHOOL for the rest of the week and he still didn't answer my calls or texts. I was planning on going over to his house if he didn't show up before the weekend but then, on the last day, there he was.

I ran up to him, tapped him on the shoulder. He turned slowly and looked at me with emo eyes.

"Hey," I said.

"Hey."

"Are you okay?"

He shrugged.

"Can we talk?"

We sat on our bench at lunch, and I noticed that he didn't have his food with him again, only an apple and some raw kale chips.

"Where's your pot?"

"I don't smoke, you know that," he said, straight-faced.

"Very funny. Not your weed."

"I didn't feel like cooking," he said. "Want some?" he handed me the bag of dry, dark green leaves.

"No thanks."

We regarded each other for a moment. "I'm sorry," I said.

He was silent.

"I miss you."

Clark nodded. After a while he said, "Me too."

Kids rushed all around us, eating and talking, and the sun was out, although the air was cool, and we had breath and heartbeats, we were alive, which was better than what Grant was. Grant, who would never have any of this ever again unless we let him. There was something intoxicating about knowing that Grant's spirit, or the part of Clark that was behaving like Grant, if that's what was going on, was so dependent on me to emerge. He had said I had helped him come back, that I had some sort of gift. This made me feel powerful and also made my stomach cower in my body, small and tight with fear. I didn't want to be able to have that much power. And mostly, I realized, I didn't want to lose my best friend.

"I think we need to figure out what to do," I said. "There's somewhere I want to go."

AFTER SCHOOL THAT DAY, Clark came over and I showed him a website I'd found for an occult store in Hollywood that had a statue of a flute-playing man with goat legs as its logo.

"No way," he said. "I'm not messing with any devil shit."

"It's not the devil, it's Pan," I said. "He's a Greek god. It's pagan."

"Whatever."

"Listen, Clark, I don't know what else to do."

Clark turned away and looked out the window. It was the one below which Grant had stood, calling my name. The wires outside buzzed with electricity, and the air was charged with the threat of rain. Then the living brother turned back to me.

Two sets of eyes in ironic black glasses confronted each other. I thought again of Grant using this body to kiss me. I had kissed Clark. And yet I hadn't. I could feel sweat pooling between my breasts in the stuffy room.

"Okay," Clark said.

THAT SATURDAY EVENING, AFTER I got off work at Treasure Hunt, we took a bus into Hollywood, although buses made Clark almost as nervous as cars (at least now I knew why), not to mention stores with "devil" logos and candles shaped like skulls, penises, and vaginas. The shop was a small, dark room stuffed with statues, amulets, herbs, and candles. I smiled cavalierly at the wax genitalia with wicks, but they made me feel uncomfortable, too. Not sure what they were for—to combat impotence, infertility, and disease, or cause them? The skull candles bothered me as much—they were so real they looked like they'd been molded on actual human skulls.

The woman behind the counter eyed us intently from under black bangs. "Possession?" she said.

I took a step away from her and looked at Clark, who seemed like he was trying to burn holes through the walls with his superhero eyes, but the woman only yawned and stretched, extending her tattoo-sleeved arms into the light and turning them to display runes, dragons, roses, and sex-crazed fairies.

"We don't know," I said.

She picked up a few white votives and set them out on

the counter. They smelled like the air before a rainstorm. Then she added a bundle of sage leaves tied with string, a packet of dried brown herbs, and a glass bottle with roses painted on the sides.

"Start with this."

"That's kind of a lot," Clark said.

The woman shrugged. "I hate to tell you this, but I see some intense shit around you. Proceed with caution, man."

"We'll just get the candles," he said.

"Okay, but if you change your mind, check this out." She handed me a small business card that I put into my purse without looking at it.

"Whatever." Clark took my arm, leading me out more forcefully than I would have expected.

"Be careful," she called after us. "He's going to take you over again and pretty soon there won't be anything left of who you were."

I tugged at my sleeves, feeling a chill so strong it made my back convulse. What secret winds cause those things?

"Nice sales pitch," Clark said. "Bad spirits. Take you over. Scare us into buying the whole f-ing store." His touch made the skin on my arm prick with excitement and his tone was fiercer than usual; for a second, I thought Grant might be there, but he wasn't. "What the hell are we supposed to do now?"

"I want to use the Ouija board again. To contact my grandmother."

He turned away from me, shaking his head, and his voice was almost a whisper. "What if he comes instead?"

An ambulance drove by, the sound ripping through the air outside like a knife across the soft flesh of my belly.

"Clark. I need to reach her," I said. "Please. I don't know what else to do. And I need you."

"Why do you need me? You could do it by yourself, right?"

"He came to us when we did it together. There's something about us, together. Maybe it could work for her, too."

"Why can I never say no to you?"

WE DIDN'T GO BACK to my house or his. We went, instead, to the house where I had once lived, the house where my grandmother died. Grant had said that she would come to us more readily there than anywhere else; maybe he was right. And asking her what to do about Grant, via the Ouija board, was the only thing I could think of.

We took the bus to Beachwood and Franklin and headed up on foot into the hills. There was my house; I still thought of it as mine. But it didn't quite feel real. I had the sensation I was watching it on a computer screen through Google Earth, a jerky satellite camera capturing every angle of the structure, the roses hacked brutally back for winter, the trees, looking shabbier now, guarding the front, the adobe roof peeking out from behind them.

I paused and stood to look at it. The sun had set and darkness in a canyon felt different from the flatlands. It seemed to fall out of the trees.

Clark moved closer. "Are you okay?"

I nodded. "Sort of. It's weird. I feel like I should be able to just open the door and walk inside."

The FOR SALE/FORECLOSURE sign was still in front. No lights were on.

"We can't, though," Clark said, as if afraid someone could hear him.

"I know. Of course not." I frowned, wishing he was bolder than I was, bold like his brother. "But we can go into the yard."

"I'm still not sure why we had to come here."

I didn't tell him it was Grant's idea. "I need to feel closer to her," I said. "When we try again."

I walked easily toward the side gate, as if I still lived in the house, and Clark followed me. The sensor light went on, as I knew it would, casting our shadows across the grass, but we slipped through quickly and the light went off. A dog barked and Clark jumped and then froze.

"It's okay, that's Marni, the neighbor's mutt." I was

tempted to call to her but realized it wasn't a good idea.

"Isn't she always close to you?" Clark asked. I realized after a second that he meant my grandmother and not the dog. His voice was trembly and I wished it wasn't. I needed him to stay steady. "I mean, wherever you are."

"Apparently not. She's not like your brother."

It wasn't a cool thing to say, and he blinked as if I'd physically startled him.

"I'm sorry," I said, but I could tell I'd lost some of his trust. I hadn't meant to hurt him; he was really all I had.

He must have had similar thoughts, because he apologized, too. "Let's just try it." He looked around at the dark garden, the empty pool illuminated by light from the street; I showed him how to avoid the sensor lights by staying at the periphery.

"It's beautiful," he said.

"I know, right?"

"I can see you here. You should still live here."

We sat together on the grass under a small fig tree with hand-like leaves. My grandmother and I used to pick the purple seedy pouches in the late summer and early fall. The lawn was damp, moisture seeping through the seat of my jeans. I took the Ouija board and the candles out of my bag. We balanced the board on our knees, and Clark lit the white candles and placed them around us on the flagstones set into the lawn. Then our fingers met on the marker.

"Grandma," I said, "I need you." I closed my eyes and thought of her wrapping her arms around me, kissing my face, braiding my hair with her small dexterous fingers. We had sat in that garden together, talking about everything. But there was so much more I wanted to tell her now and, more important, so much I wanted to ask.

"Grandma," I said again, inhaling the night, the air of the hills, which was different from the air in the lower regions of the city, because feral animals lurked nearer and wild plants grew unchecked. I could also smell the drop of her lavender oil I had applied to one of my wrists and the drop of Shalimar I had applied to the other, cherishing them like the essences of precious jewels because they had belonged to her, touched her skin.

I didn't open my eyes. My hands stayed steady on the marker. "Is this you?"

Though my eyes were closed, I could see, through my lids, the candles flare around me.

The marker slid haltingly across the board. I opened my eyes to look.

Just then we heard a police siren in the distance and dogs barking. Clark blew out the candles and jumped up. "Let's get out of here, Julie!" he said. "I don't feel okay about this. It's trespassing."

"Wait," I snapped. There was no way I was stopping then. "Not yet."

"Do you want to get arrested?"

Damn. "Okay, okay." I got up, too, suddenly realizing Clark was probably right about coming here, flashing on a dream I'd had—had I dreamed this?—of being at this house, of red lights and sirens and danger. Grant's idea could have gotten us in jail. *Grant,* I thought. What if he took over Clark entirely? Where would Clark be then? The police weren't all I was afraid of.

CLARK AND I DIDN'T mention the Ouija board or Grant or my grandmother again for a few days. I think we just needed a rest from the whole thing. Grant didn't show up. I had the bizarre, and palpably chilly sensation that he, too, was resting, or just laying low, trying to make us miss him, like a girl playing hard to get when she was afraid of being dumped. If we missed him enough, we wouldn't want to send him away.

I did miss him, if I was honest, the urgent way he had looked at me as if I alone had the power to bring him back to life. The way I felt less—but also more—alive when I was with him, like I was escaping all the worries and fears and floating in a dream. But he scared me, too. I tried not to think about any of it.

My birthday was the next week, and my mom took

Clark and me out for frozen yogurt, and we rented *Harry Potter and the Goblet of Fire*, our mutual favorite of the series. I got a cerise wool beret from Clark and a card from my mother.

Birthdays at the old house, when my grandmother was alive, were big deals, with elaborate three-course meals on china and homemade cakes covered in fresh roses and sparkling lemonade in champagne glasses with gold rims and twinkle lights in the trees and lots of presents that my grandmother wrapped in rose-covered paper and tied with raffia and pink satin. I thanked my mother as graciously as I could for the card and the movie and dessert, but inside I felt a little anger demon jumping up and down on one foot and shaking his fist at her, reminding me, once again, how much everything had changed.

SOMETHING ELSE HAD CHANGED. After Clark left that night, my mom told me that she and Luke would be going up north together for Thanksgiving in a few days and that I could come along.

"What the hell?" I said. "You're acting like you're engaged. You just met him two months ago."

She ignored me. "I thought it would be a nice change. We need to get away. There's a cute bed-and-breakfast Luke knows about."

"Where am I supposed to sleep? And what about Thanksgiving? We always cook!" I felt a shudder of anger so strong, I thought it might make something combust inside me.

"You'll have your own room, of course," she said. "I thought it would be better to do something different. Now that Grandma's gone." She bit her lip and fanned her face as if she might start crying. "I'm sorry, honey. If you want, I won't go."

I left her sitting at the kitchen table, slammed the door to my room, and called Clark.

"What are you doing on Thanksgiving?" I asked. "Because basically if I have to spend it at a bed-and-breakfast with my mother and the boyfriend, I am basically going to hurl."

"You can have it with us," he said.

"Are you sure it's okay? I know they don't like company."

"They'll deal," he said. "This is important. It'll be good for them. And you can't be alone on a holiday."

But my mom wasn't concerned about leaving me alone. She simply said, "I know you'll be in good hands with Clark and his family."

On Wednesday evening, she was packed and waiting for Luke in the living room. She had on her usual tight jeans and heels, a sprinkling of glitter on her cheeks this time. It was getting into the creases around her eyes and made her look older.

"Is that my glitter powder?"

She touched her face. "Oh, yes. I thought it would be okay. I'm sorry."

"It's not okay," I said. "And it looks like you're trying to be seventeen or something."

My mom bit her lip and blinked her eyes and her whole body stiffened. I could tell I'd hurt her feelings, but I reminded myself that she was the one who was leaving me alone on Thanksgiving.

"You don't have to speak to me like that. And besides, I bought you that glitter, if I recall," she said.

"When you had a job! When you had a life, instead of hanging out with this aging rocker freak."

"Stop it, just stop it, Julie."

I turned away and went to my room.

I heard Luke's truck in the street. My mom didn't even bother to say good-bye when she left. And she didn't call me all that night or even the next day.

THANKSGIVING NIGHT, STILL NOT having heard from her, I dragged myself out of bed, where I'd been reading, and into the shower, then put on a light-blue cashmere beaded cardigan sweater that had belonged to my grandma, a black skirt, blue-and-gray argyle slouchy socks, and black ankle strap shoes, added my grandmother's black satin bow-shaped purse, and walked over to Clark's house with a bottle of sparkling apple cider. I hadn't really felt like leaving my room, let alone the apartment, but I made myself; the idea of being alone was the only thing worse than having to get dressed and go out.

Clark answered the door in his usual jeans and Chucks but also wearing a white dress shirt, green tie, and the argyle sweater he'd bought at Treasure Hunt. He looked like a little old man, except young and tall. I guess he felt the tie made up for the lack of hat.

"You look nice, dude," I said, trying to sound cheerful.

He blushed along his jawline. "You too."

The house smelled like a holiday, the way our house used to smell this time of year. Cinnamon, nutmeg, cloves, vanilla, a turkey baking in the oven. Clark's living room felt warm and cozy with soft sofas and a fire in the fireplace. I looked for pictures of Clark and a boy who looked just like him, but more handsome, no glasses, slightly more muscular build, maybe some of him posed in his basketball jersey, with his team. Maybe some sports trophies.

There wasn't anything.

Clark's mom came in wearing a vintage cotton apron printed with large colorful fruits.

"Hi, I'm Lisa."

"Hi," I said. "Nice apron."

"Oh, thank you." She was tall and thin like her boys, with sad eyes. I wondered if her eyes and Clark's had been sad before Grant died. When Grant came, his eyes never looked sad—just hungry. I shook my head to knock the thought of him out of the way.

"Clark's said a lot of nice things about you."

I wanted to return the compliment, but I realized that he never really mentioned his family. I assumed that it was because he was afraid it might lead to Grant.

Awkward. "Thanks," I managed.

"Can we help you with dinner?" Clark asked her.

The kitchen was small and brightly lit, with blue ceramic pots that I recognized; they matched the one Clark carried around in his backpack. "So this is where you learned to cook," I said to him, watching his mother baste the bird. "Your son's a really good chef."

She laughed. "A little healthier than I am, I'm afraid."

"Where'd you get so into all the healthy stuff anyway, Clark?" I asked him as I tossed the salad.

He shook his head and spooned vegan pumpkin-pie filling into a coconut-and-almond-meal piecrust he had made. "Just another example of my neurosis."

"In that case, never get over it."

His dad came in, also tall and thin, balding, and wearing glasses. He greeted me with a quick handshake. I decided the sad eyes weren't genetic but had come upon all of them in the last couple of years.

"Hello, I'm Hal. Nice to meet you."

"You too," I said. "You have really great sons." How had I made that slip? *Damn.* "Son. A really great son."

He didn't show that it had bothered him, but I was sure it did by the way the air suddenly felt stormy—heavy and electric.

"Well, I'm going to catch some football." He excused himself, and Clark watched him go. I knew what he was thinking. If Grant were there, Grant would be invited in to watch the game, not Clark, the less favored, less athletic son. The son who cooked. And thinking like that only brought on guilt and remorse. *Why wasn't I the one who died?*

Maybe I'm wrong, I told myself. *I can't read Clark's mind.*

We drowned our worries for a while with food. There was green salad with persimmons, pumpkin soup, turkey, cranberry-orange sauce, buttered-green-bean-and-almond casserole, homemade bread with butter, and Clark's extreme vegan pie that even his parents had to admit was surprisingly delicious. I was so full afterward that I could hardly move. Clark asked if I wanted to go up to his room after we'd helped with the dishes, but I could tell the idea made him nervous and he was only being polite, so I asked if he'd drive me home instead. I knew he wasn't big on driving, but I figured it wasn't that far and it wouldn't hurt him to get used to it, especially if he ever wanted a semblance of a social life.

The night was cold and quiet; everyone was away on their fancy vacations. I thought of my mom and Luke in bed in a room with quaint wallpaper and cuckoo clocks on the walls. I could see his bare, white feet sticking out from under the patchwork quilt.

I was grateful to be with Clark, to be with the living brother. When we pulled up in front of my apartment, I fished around in my purse for my keys, and my fingers caught in the torn silk lining, grazing a small card. I pulled it out and read:

black jade herbs and acupuncture

And in smaller letters:

DAIYU KAUFMAN

WE SPECIALIZE IN CONTACTING SPIRIT WORLD, SPIRIT POSSESSION.

It was the card the woman at the occult store had given me, but it felt as if it had found my fingers in the purse, rather than the other way around. The address was in Chinatown.

I tucked the card into a zippered pocket of the purse for safe-keeping.

Clark and I said a hurried good night and I didn't invite him in.

I WOKE LATER TO a banging sound that practically lifted me off my mattress. *What the hell?* The digital clock read 12:03. For some reason this in itself bothered me, but I didn't know why.

I froze, staring at the phone across the room, unable to move toward it.

The bang again. A shuddering bang. Coming from the kitchen. The door of my room opened and I shot out of bed.

"Honey?" The light flipped on. My mom was standing in my room in a black silk slip I hadn't seen before. "Are you okay?"

"You scared the shit out of me. When did you get here? What was that?"

"Luke's going to see."

He came in behind her, shirtless in his black jeans. I looked away and covered my chest with the blanket.

"It's just the refrigerator," Luke said. "It's a piece of crap. You should tell your landlord."

I didn't think the refrigerator was broken. It had never done that before. The sound was angry, as if it was trying to tell me something. Vague thoughts scratched in the back of my mind, like rats, bits of information that I couldn't quite trap.

Luke put his arm around my mom and drew her toward him.

"I'll be right in," she said, pushing gently on his chest, and he left my room.

Then she came and sat on my bed. She looked fragile, as though she'd rattle if you shook her. "Are you okay?" she asked again.

I glared at her. "When did you get back?"

"A few hours ago. I felt badly leaving you and about our fight. I'm so sorry. Did you have fun at Clark's?"

I could smell Luke's odor on her. "Don't let him in my room," I said, turning my back and throwing myself down onto the sagging mattress.

She stayed there for a few more minutes, then sighed and left. I would have preferred the bang of the refrigerator all night over the sound of Luke's band's CD or, even worse, the sound of their voices through the wall.

THE NEXT DAY I rested and tried to numb myself with reality TV and the leftovers Clark's mom had sent home with me, avoiding my mom and Luke until I went to sleep around ten that night.

I dreamed I was with Grant in the sepia ancestor world again. He was holding my hand, leading me somewhere through misty rooms with potted palms and wicker chairs. A large china doll with glass eyes sat on a velvet love seat, watching me. I was cold, so cold, and I couldn't get warm.

"Where are we?" I asked Grant.

A woman was sitting at a table covered with a cloth. For some reason it disturbed me that I could not see the legs of the table. There was a large crystal ball in front of her, and a fox with glass eyes was draped around her neck.

I heard Grant's voice: "You wanted to know what it was like. This is what it is like."

"What what's like?"

The table at which the woman sat was skidding slowly across the floor.

"Be with me and all this can be yours," Grant said, sweeping his hand across the cold, brown-paper landscape, a painted mural of a garden, populated by stern, sad, one-dimensional beings with the eyes of mystics.

I looked down at my arm. The red tattoo from the other dream was there again. I could make out the letters this time.

E
V
I
L

The pounding of my own heart woke me like a knock at the door. My covers had fallen off, the window had blown open, and the night air bit. I shivered as if I was still inside the dream. What did it mean? What was evil? Who was evil? Was it a message from Grant?

Or about him?

I knew I needed to find out and the only clue I had was the card in my purse: BLACK JADE.

The next morning I called Clark and told him that I wanted to go to Chinatown the following Saturday and try to learn more about the strange things that were happening to us.

BLACK JADE

2

I attempted to make the week pass as quickly as possible by staying busy at work and, when I was home, studying, reading, or looking through the clothing and purses and jewelry and photos that had belonged to my grandmother as if I were going to find some new clue that would bring her closer to me and help us deal with Grant. Nothing.

I realized how isolated I had become; I had no interest in seeing anyone besides Mrs. Carol and Clark, and he and I had decided it was better not to be alone together for a while, until we had a better plan. It was hard to imagine that I'd wanted to attend Ally Kellogg's north-of-Wilshire party a month ago.

And now, the refrigerator had begun to bang every night,

and I found I reacted more fearfully than seemed appropriate, startling as if a bomb had gone off and then wondering why it frightened me so much. I wished Clark was there to defend me from the evil fridge, but I wasn't sure he could defend me from anything.

When I finally stepped outside into the bright December light that Saturday, wearing a red Chinese silk dress and black Doc Martens, and my hair secured into a bun with chopsticks, I cowered a little, wanting to go back inside and hide in spite of the possibility that Luke might be coming to visit.

Clark drove his mom's car but anxiously, leaning forward over the steering wheel and braking suddenly like an old person.

"You okay?" I asked him.

"Yeah. I really don't like to drive that much."

"I know. That's what I meant." I put my hand on his arm and then drew it away quickly, worried I would stimulate Grant that way. Clark's skin was warm and smooth; I could almost feel the blood moving through his veins.

We arrived in Chinatown, parked, and walked through the plaza. It was unseasonably hot and sticky, and we tried to stay in the shade of the buildings.

"What's up with this heat?" I said.

Clark frowned and ripped at a cuticle with his teeth. "Global warming? Remember what I said about cold weather making people more friendly? One day the world will be so hot no one will ever even want to speak to each other again."

The hot, antagonistic air danced with red paper lanterns, and dragons were inlaid into the pavement under our feet. Clark and I saw jade Buddhas, and rose-quartz Quan Yins, table fountains that lit up in neon, bonsai trees, and bamboo in dragon-shaped planters.

I remembered coming to Chinatown once with my grandmother; she had bought me a little purse of pink Chinese silk and a gold silk lipstick case with red cherry blossoms on it and a tiny rectangular mirror inside. Then we'd eaten steamed dumplings. I could see her face, smiling at me in the small, fragrant, dimly lit restaurant as she taught me to use the chopsticks that she'd tied together with a ribbon to make it easier.

Clark bought a Chinese straw hat, of course, and he got me a purple paper parasol with a fake jade pendant on the handle; he thought I might be getting too much sun, and I couldn't bring myself to wear a hat when I was around him—overkill.

Black Jade, the Chinese herb store, had large glass canisters full of candy in front and shelves of cosmetics enhanced with ground pearls. It was hard to get through the narrow, crowded aisles to the section in the back.

We parted the piece of silk that hung across the door. The room was practically closet sized, filled with statues and large glass jars of dried and gnarled roots. I breathed in sweet incense and acrid herbs. The woman behind the counter scowled at us.

"Do you need something?"

"Are you Daiyu?"

She leaned forward, scrutinizing me. Her hair was spiked with gel, and her nose was pierced. She smelled like the white jasmine flowers that grew over the back wall of our old house, and biting black tea that made your heart beat faster in the morning. A faint silver light was coming off her, and I thought again of my grandmother's lavender color, my mother's gray, the green I'd seen when I first met Clark. I hadn't noticed anything like this for a while and it still made me feel strange, almost like I was in someone else's body. Finally the woman nodded and we introduced ourselves.

"I'm trying to reach my grandmother," I told her.

"There's not just a grandmother," she said, eyeing Clark.

He and I exchanged looks but didn't say anything.

Daiyu nodded. "It's an angry ghost."

Clark was glaring now. "I can't believe these people," he muttered. "Bad spirits. Angry ghosts. Good way to make a buck."

I elbowed him.

"This isn't simple," she said.

"Is there something we can do?" I asked her.

"Not much you can do for a despairing ghost. Devastation and emptiness. You can try Matawhero Magic rose, Iris Gee rose, Arethusa rose. To help combat unwanted entities."

I saw Clark out of the corner of my eye, flexing his hands.

"That's all?" I asked.

"You use mugwort. I sell that one. Just don't eat it or let it touch your skin for too long; it's toxic."

"Like Hogwarts?" Clark said, and I heard the *s* whistle. "Uh, get it? Harry Potter?"

Thankfully Daiyu ignored his joke. "You'll also need Salvia dorrii. Light white candles. Sometimes more is required." She shrugged. "It's all about overcoming your fear and grief. Letting go. Nothing really works until then."

"What's *Salvia* . . . ?" I asked.

"A less common breed of desert sagebrush." Daiyu frowned at us—Clark with his straw hat, me with my parasol, like silly tourists, standing there in the smoky room, facing her. It was so dark and cool in the store, hard to imagine that the sun shone hot outside.

"I'm not sure I'm going to sell it to you, actually." She ran her hand over the spikes of hair on top of her head. Her arms were thin, but their muscles looked surprisingly strong.

"Why not?" It suddenly seemed urgent. *Devastation and*

emptiness. I thought of Grant in my dream. Was he the ghost of despair? A dead boy who wanted what he could never have?

"How do I know you're serious? Let alone able?"

"We're serious," I promised her, meeting her gaze without flinching, though I wanted to. I wasn't sure about the able part.

"We'll see." She paused, scrutinizing us some more, looking past—I hoped—the hat and parasol. "You want acupuncture treatments? For free for you both. I can read your energy and decide if I want to sell you the herbs."

We exchanged a quick glance. This lady was tough. I wondered (a little contemptuously, I realized) if Clark was afraid of needles.

"Sure, why not?" I said, and we followed her into an even smaller, darker room, where I sat on a table, and Clark took the chair. Incense burned to ash, and small stone statues on a shelf watched me serenely. Daiyu checked my tongue and pressed two fingers into my wrist to feel my pulse.

"Have you had a treatment before?"

I shook my head.

"Been here before?"

"Once. To Chinatown." Suddenly it felt as though salt water was simmering inside me, pinching at my sinuses and tear ducts.

"You're thinking of your grandmother, right?"

I nodded, afraid to open my mouth for fear of sobbing.

"You miss her?"

I nodded again. Couldn't speak.

"She's here with you. You just have to keep open to her."

"But she won't come," I said. "I tried. That's how all this started." I waited, tensing my legs so hard that my calves cramped. Maybe Daiyu had the answer.

But all she said was, "You try too hard. Let go. Relax and allow the energy to shift and open in your body." She briskly pierced me with the tiny needles, but so quickly and lightly, with such a steady hand, that I hardly flinched; they were less sharp than her eyes.

"Weird things happened when she died," I said. "I mean, right when she died. Colors and sounds and then some dreams."

"Auras," said Daiyu. "The energy of people. You can bridge the worlds. You're an intuitive, I think. Sometimes these gifts are passed down."

"What?" I tried to sit up but she wouldn't let me. She was really strong. "You think my grandma could . . . could see stuff?"

"Not her. Your father."

"My father? He was a sperm donor. I never even knew him."

Daiyu shrugged. "You relax," she said. "You'll learn slowly."

"But what does it mean? What do I do with it?"

"You relax now." Daiyu looked hard at me, and I closed my eyes and felt myself drifting softly away from the room, the city, into a place where soft fog drifted over shallow water and plants grew up out of it. I saw slender birds sail across the sky and I heard whispering voices, women singing. I could smell wood smoke and wet leaves, and a warm tingling sensation pulsed through my body. I felt more peaceful than I had since we'd lost Grandma and left the house.

A figure was moving toward me, a figure made out of a lavender light and a great kindness, but the next thing I knew, I heard Daiyu's voice calling me back and the figure retreated. I wanted to reach out for her, call for her to return, but she was gone.

I sat up unsteadily. Clark was watching me, his forehead corrugated with worry. "Is there anything more you can tell me?" I asked the proprietor of Black Jade. Which, I realized, was the color of her eyes.

She helped me off the table, placing her hands on my back and steering me out. "That's all I can say. You need to discover for yourself." She handed me a small yellow glass bottle with a dropper. "Take this. Four drops in the morning and at night. It will help. But it must come from you."

"What else do you know?" I said. "Please." I was so far away from the foggy river world to where I had traveled during my treatment, and from the glowing figure I had wanted to touch.

Daiyu shook her head again. "That's all. Now it's your friend's turn."

Half an hour later Clark's treatment was complete and Daiyu handed him his own orange glass bottle. I was a little surprised he had gone so willingly, in spite of his skepticism.

"I gave you a lung treatment," Daiyu told me. "A kidney one for him. Lungs govern grief in Chinese medicine, and kidney is fear. You'll both be more prepared now for your work."

But what was that work? we both were wondering.

Daiyu, evidently convinced that we were worthy of the herb if not more information, sold us the mugwort and told us two places where we might possibly find the roses, but would say no more.

AFTER LEAVING DAIYU, WE went to a restaurant and ordered soup and rice and plump, delicate-skinned steamed dumplings, which we ate carefully with chopsticks, trying not to let the cabbage and tofu fall out onto the crane-and-cherry-blossom-painted plates. I shivered in the air-conditioned restaurant and wished I'd brought a sweater. One that belonged to my grandmother. Maybe black cashmere and bugle-beaded with a note in the pocket quoting a famous poem.

Clark shook the small plastic bag I'd set on the table. "What's this toxic warthog stuff anyway?"

"Mugwort," I said.

"I don't get it. I can't see how any of this is going to work." I couldn't help but think that he really meant, *I don't want this to work. Not yet.* "And how do we know this lady is legit?"

"She seemed to know stuff," I told him. About the ghost, the auras, the treatments we needed.

"Yeah, and what's this with auras?"

I shrugged and looked down, suddenly embarrassed. Maybe I did just have a brain disorder.

"Sorry," Clark said. "This shit is just a lot to take."

"But you're a *Buffy* fan. You shouldn't be upset by a little aura," I tried to joke.

"Remember I told you, fiction versus nonfiction." He frowned. "Do you really see them?"

"I saw this lavender color when my grandma died. It was so strong. And just now, Daiyu, she was sort of silver?"

"What color am I?" Clark asked, his eyes big behind his glasses.

"Green. Bright, clear, light green."

"Cool." Clark smiled and I was relieved. "That makes me think about trees," he said. "And you know where they have a lot of trees, right?"

I could tell he was on board now. It had just taken a reference to his favorite TV show and the mention of the right color. He was surprisingly easy to cheer up for someone who could be so brooding.

WE DROVE OUT TO Arcadia, to the Arboretum, one of the places where Daiyu said we might be able to track down the rare roses. Pathways led us among tall trees, past a lagoon, where ducks swam under wide palms. There was a small bent-willow-branch hut that we had to stoop to enter.

"I want to live here," I said, wistful as a willow.

Across the lawn was a boarded-up Victorian Queen Anne–style house, painted red and white with lacy trim, spires, and a wraparound porch. Peacocks paraded across the lawn like cloisonné statues come to life.

"Okay. I'll live there," Clark said, pointing to the house. "You can come over when you want to shower."

"Hey, no fair." I softly slapped his shoulder. The mood had changed suddenly among the trees, to something even lighter than when we had left the restaurant, and I could tell we both needed that.

He pulled my hair, gently, tugging the braid down my

back. It was the most he'd ever really touched me, as Clark. I laughed and grabbed his straw hat from his head. He chased me out of the willow hut, through the gardens, among the vine-covered arbors. Peacocks ignored us, fanning their tails narcissistically, oblivious. We were forgetting why we had come.

Until a shadow passed over the sun and we stood on the path under a large, flowering tree, looking at each other. For a second, I thought I saw Grant flashing behind Clark's eyes and then he was gone.

The rose garden was severely pruned, leaving only thorny stems, and we couldn't even find the autumn skeletons of the three bushes we were looking for. I wondered for a moment if Daiyu was messing with us.

Still, it had been a good day. I felt better for having gotten out. I thought of Colin and Mary, the sickly, peevish children in *The Secret Garden*, a book my grandma had liked to read to me when I was little. How it was the natural world outside the house, behind the gates, among the crocuses and roses that healed them. For me, the house we lived in when I was growing up was a secret garden, inside and out.

Clark and I drove home in silence.

Finally he said, "I'm not sure I want this."

He leaned back from the steering wheel and un-hunched his shoulders. "Even though this whole thing is fucking weird. I don't know; part of me is still glad he is using my body, that he's with me somehow."

I nodded, trying not to give away too much of my own ambivalence.

"But it still freaks me out, too." He paused. "She called him emptiness and . . . what was it?"

"Devastation."

His shoulders shivered; I couldn't tell if it was spontaneous or if he was consciously shaking something off.

"We at least need to go to the other address she gave us for the roses," I said.

CLARK TOLD ME GOOD-BYE in front of my apartment.

"Do you want to come in?" I asked him.

He glanced over his shoulder, as if he expected someone to be there, watching us. "No, it's okay," he mumbled, and I realized he was afraid that Grant might come.

I pretended to feel relieved that Clark hadn't come in, that Grant couldn't visit, but to be honest I wanted company. The day had been the best one I'd had in a long time and it was hard to transition back to the empty apartment. My mom was out and there was nothing to eat. Luckily I was still full from the giant lunch I'd had with Clark. I took a bubble bath, put Daiyu's tincture under my tongue, got in bed with *To the Lighthouse*, and fell asleep around eleven.

The refrigerator woke me with a bang just after midnight, like a warning. The landlord had checked it out but couldn't find anything wrong and this made me even more uneasy.

I got up to get a glass of water from the filter bottle inside and a noxious smell hit me so hard it was almost three-dimensional. Covering my mouth with one hand, I looked around for the source but couldn't see anything, so I went to bed with the windows open. In the morning, the kitchen was freezing cold but the smell was gone.

THAT WEEK AT SCHOOL was uneventful. My mother job-hunted during the day and went out for dinner with Luke most nights, coming home late with her leftovers for my next dinner. I tried to focus on work and school. Ms. Merritt's class was the easiest because I could escape into poetry. I planned to do my report that was due after Christmas vacation on Emily Dickinson, if I could gather the courage to pick up my grandmother's Dickinson book—it reminded me too much of the day she had died.

Daiyu's tincture, which I took three times a day, eased some of the sadness I felt, at least for a little while. Maybe it was my imagination, but it seemed I could breathe a bit more freely every time I used it.

Clark didn't come over, but we saw each other in class

and had lunch together. As we ate his *kicharee*, we planned for the next Sunday when we would go to see Tatiana González, the second source Daiyu had suggested for the roses we needed. Though we still weren't exactly sure how we were going to use them.

CASA FLORIBUNDA

3

"*I hate that they* call this the 'Suicide Bridge,'" Clark said, clinging to the steering wheel as he drove us over the bridge to Pasadena.

"Have you been taking your drops?" I asked him.

"Yeah, all week. I don't know if they're working."

"Well, at least you're not at home with your head under the covers," I said, and he smiled.

"At least you're not turning goth, only wearing black, and listening to The Cure all day," he countered.

Maybe Clark was becoming less afraid and I was a little less depressed. Or maybe we were imagining it, but I still felt glad to be crossing the bridge, out in the day, away from our regular indoor lives. I could breathe better, even on a bridge called Suicide.

We had called Tatiana González and mentioned Daiyu, and Tatiana had told us to come. She hadn't asked any questions, but there had been a knowing tone to her voice that made me think she might be able to help us.

Tatiana lived in a huge, pale-pink Spanish adobe overgrown with entwined purple morning glories and red bougainvillea. It reminded me a little of our old house, except much bigger, sprawling for a good portion of the tree-and-mansion-lined block behind an adobe wall and wrought-iron gate with the words *Casa Floribunda* written in script. Also, this house had silver *milagros*—charms of hands, feet, legs, lips, eyes, and hearts—embedded in almost every inch of the outer front walls.

I was glad I had worn a turquoise cotton 1950s skirt, covered with silver sparkles, with my black-and-turquoise cowboy boots and T-shirt—it seemed to go with the setting. A scent of flowers, so strong it felt as if I were holding a bouquet to my nose, met us as we walked inside the courtyard. I could hear the play of water from small fountains and wind chimes that seemed to be singing specifically to us.

A petite woman, black curls adorned with fresh gardenias and cascading to her minuscule waist, met us at the door in a burst of indigo light. Either my perceptions of color, or auras as Daiyu had called them, were becoming

stronger, or hers and Daiyu's were just particularly notice-
able, which made sense.

"Welcome!" The woman hugged us both and kissed
our cheeks. I saw Clark blush, and a tiny wince of jealousy
passed through me. I realized I cared about what Clark felt
for other women more than I had thought.

We followed her into the house. The floors were tiled,
and the walls glowed in soft colors, different for every room.
Pale apricot, smoke blue, lavender. Gleaming oil paintings
in antique frames hung everywhere, and there were many
elaborately carved wooden figures with beads and dried
rose wreaths around their necks. Tatiana took us into a sitting room overlooking a small orchard of fruit trees. There
was tea set out for us, along with tamarind ices and guava
cream-cheese pastries.

"Tell me about yourselves," Tatiana said. She wore a
purple silk blouse, jeans, and high-heeled sandals, one of
which she rocked on the end of her foot as she observed us.

"We're seniors at Beverly Hills High. We heard about
you from Daiyu."

"Not that. I mean, what is really happening. There's
some kind of obstacle, no?"

I always felt weird mentioning Grant, as if he could hear
me, so I just said, "We're trying to reach my grandmother.
She died last August."

"I'm sorry to hear that. But there's something more, too?"

"Clark's brother, Grant," I said.

"And this Grant, he's no longer with us either."

I shook my head no.

"I'm so sorry," Tatiana said, to Clark this time.

"Thank you." Clark's voice cracked.

Our hostess regarded us with her dark, almond-shaped eyes, then poured the tea. It had a woodsy fragrance, and I let the steam permeate my skin.

"It's so hard, death," Tatiana said. "We aren't taught or prepared. It's hard to let someone go, especially when they aren't ready either." She looked directly at Clark and twirled a large ring on her finger. "Sometimes we want more of them after they leave, but sometimes, no matter how much we love them, we want less."

Clark dropped his head and looked at his hands. Tatiana went on.

"My mother died and I was haunted by her spirit for three years. She would overtake me and I'd come to in the strangest places. I was exhausted all the time and lost weight. I weighed eighty pounds. I couldn't send her away. The idea of having her so close again was—was like an elixir, *embriagador*, intoxicating, even though I was never present to experience it. She came to be with Florian."

A puckish man in his twenties was standing in the arched doorway behind her and she greeted him without turning around. "Hello, Florian. I was just talking about you."

He walked toward us as if he were on a fashion runway, lifting foot over foot, kicking up his heels, wearing a tight, well-fitted suit with slightly short pants that skimmed the tops of his shiny shoes. There was an ascot around his neck, and his blond-streaked hair was swept to the side over enormous brown eyes fanned by long lashes.

"This is my son, Florian."

She looked much too young to be his mom. Tatiana smiled as Florian shook our hands. "Isn't she great?" He beamed. "Pleased to meet you. Grandmother said you'd be coming."

We looked at Tatiana González, who explained, "Before she finally left us for good, she told him lots of things."

Florian nodded. "We don't share this information with everyone. Some people are a bit bothered by it. But we think you understand."

"She has some talents, yes?" Tatiana was staring at me, but not meeting my eyes; her gaze was at the very center of my forehead. "You see the colors, Julie?"

I hesitated; for a moment I wasn't sure if she was talking to me or not, even though she'd said my name. "You mean, around people, right? Sometimes."

She twirled the ring on her finger the other way. "May I ask if you see mine?"

The indigo light was pulsing stronger now. "Blue," I said shyly. Clark looked at me with what I could only describe as tender wonder. "But I don't always see them," I said. "I only saw my mom's once, when she was really depressed, and I saw Clark's when we met."

"Being able to see auras can be developed. You need to practice. It can help you in your life. It can help you know whom to trust and not to trust." She took the ring off her finger, reached for my hand, and slipped it on mine. I wondered how it could fit; her fingers seemed much smaller. "This will help," she said, "for you to see the colors."

It resembled a cheap mood ring, the kind that had gone in and out of style more than once, but when I looked into the milky surface of the ring and then held it toward Tatiana, the stone shone with indigo undertones.

Clark and I exchanged a glance. I wasn't sure he was entirely comfortable with all this.

Tatiana held up a finger, gesturing for us to wait, went into another room, and came back with a book. It was titled *How to Read and Understand Auras* and had illustrations with little figures surrounded by different shades, as well as charts with colored circles and dark dots.

"You need to develop your peripheral vision with these

exercises," Tatiana said. "It will help. The front of the retina is more damaged from overuse. You will see better from the side. But this, this understanding of the colors, isn't why you came, is it?"

"We're looking for some roses," I told her. Although part of me wondered if that much information was necessary; she and her son seemed to know everything about our visit already.

"Well, you've come to the right place!" Florian exclaimed. He and Tatiana took us out some glass doors into a garden filled with flowers. The scent in the air, as Florian described it, was "positively ambrosial." I was happy to have come if for nothing more than to smell that fragrance.

"They bloom like that this time of year?" I asked. It was early December; roses were pruned now, weren't they?

"Here they do." Without asking the names of the flowers we needed, he led us straight to three rosebushes planted side by side near a white lattice trellis covered with bell-shaped lilies.

The Magic Matawhero, pale-gold floribunda, so fragrant it made me feel drunk, the pink, charmingly blowsy Iris Gee rose, and the precise petaled apricot Arethusa rose.

Clark and I stood staring at the flowers after I had sniffed each one.

"How much are these?"

"They're a gift, right, Mother? More grow the more we pick." Tatiana nodded, and Florian went on, "You can purchase some essences if you'd like. But we love to share the flowers with people who understand. So many people don't understand."

A soft breeze plundered the rosebushes as he spoke and shook blossoms onto the pathway.

"I think someone besides us wants you to have them," Florian said, stooping to pick them up and hand them to me. One two three. "Wind spirit."

"Wash the petals and put them in a pot of distilled water with cinnamon, simmer until they lose their color," Tatiana said. "Let it cool, strain the water, put it in a spray bottle, and refrigerate it."

In my mind, I heard my refrigerator bang, and shuddered involuntarily.

"It all depends on what exactly you're dealing with," she went on. "*Espíritu maligno*? Or something else. Unfortunately I can't diagnose that. It can only come from you. When you are ready. But you might meet resistance."

Was she talking about Grant? *Espíritu maligno* didn't sound good. Clark nibbled his cuticles; I could tell he was as frustrated with the whole conversation as I was. But we still purchased two tiny glass bottles of flower-and-gem essences Tatiana had made herself. Star of Bethlehem, rock rose, and aspen mixed with obsidian for Clark. Gentian, gray spider flower, hornbeam, and dog rose with clear quartz and amethyst for me.

"You need to feel more joy," she said. "Not give up on life. *Sí*, I think so. And the quartz and amethyst are to help develop your psychic abilities. For your friend?" She looked at Clark, who blushed. "More self-confidence. Less fear."

I heard him whisper, "Not again."

Ignoring Clark, I patted some of the essence onto the inside of my wrist. "You too," I said, and he did the same, but he didn't look too happy about it.

As we were about to leave, I turned to Tatiana. "Is there anything else you can tell us?" I asked. "Please."

A worried look rippled the placid surface of her face, a breeze on deep blue-violet water. "You have the roses. And the essences. The book and the ring. The rest I can't tell you. It must come from . . ."

"Yeah, from us, we know," Clark said.

Tatiana shook her head, so the curls moved like small, shiny clusters of grapes. She put her hands on my shoulders and looked into my eyes. "I gave you what I could. I can't tell you any more than that. I'm sorry."

Clark and I walked out of Casa Floribunda with mysterious gifts and unanswered questions, as if the house were a fairyland, a place we didn't want to leave but knew if we didn't, we would get lost there forever.

We got in the car and sat in silence for a while. I noticed his leg was jiggling.

"How about we shoot some hoops at my house?" he said.

"What?" I looked up, trying to see if Grant was there. No sign of him.

"I don't know. She said you needed to feel more joy or whatever. We could get some dinner and then play basketball."

"You're sure?"

He ignored the worry in my voice. Seemed like Tatiana's essences were already working. "Yeah. I used to play. As a kid. I just was never like him."

So we drove back over Suicide Bridge to get some takeout Vietnamese pho noodles in broth with fresh herbs and some fresh-squeezed limeade and then went back to Clark's house. His parents weren't there. We ate the food and then we shot baskets in the driveway until the sun went down in the west to the rhythm of the ball on the cement, and the sky behind the palm trees was streaked with quickly fading pink light.

I was relieved to see how bad Clark was at the game and that we were both laughing.

Grant didn't show.

❧

I ALMOST INVITED CLARK in but I thought better of it, worried that Grant might come after all. He seemed to have a preference for visiting me at night in my room.

So I was alone when I simmered the roses in a pot of boiling distilled water, added a cinnamon stick, strained it, and put it into a spray bottle in the refrigerator when it cooled, as Tatiana had instructed me. I also tried to use the eye charts she'd given me and I took the herbal tincture from Daiyu and applied Tatiana's gem essences.

But as I'd told Clark, I didn't know what else to do.

Lighting white candles in my dark room, I asked the Ouija board again, but nothing happened. The marker sat leadenly on the board. Not even a NO.

"Grandma," I called, crying in my bed, my face pushed into a lavender sachet I'd found in her jewelry box, wanting her comfort, her wisdom, the safe space of her arms.

"Grandma!"

The Emily Dickinson poem I had read to her the day she died was reciting itself in my head. "A Visitor in Marl."

I got up and took the book off my shelf for the first time since that day. When I opened it, a piece of paper fell out. I was surprised I hadn't seen it on the day my grandmother died, but I might not have paid any attention to it then if I had. Death can give significance to every detail that came before.

Unfolding the piece of paper, I saw it was an advertisement for a store in Joshua Tree, California. ED RAINWATER DESIGNS. Apparently the shop sold small, carved bone figures, dream catchers, jewelry. And one more thing—the thing we needed: sage. Of the somewhat rare *Salvia dorrii* variety.

As I read the word, the refrigerator banged louder than ever and the walls of the apartment shook. It was 12:03. Again. I shuddered almost as violently as the appliance, realizing that this was always the time of the banging. I went into the kitchen. The same vile smell was in the air.

Why did my grandmother have this advertisement? And why had I found it now when *Salvia dorrii* was exactly what Clark and I needed?

I was going to wake my mother and tell her, when Luke came in behind me, wearing a bathrobe, swearing at the refrigerator. I glanced down at Tatiana's ring on my finger. It was a disgusting bile-green color. I looked at Luke and the same ugly green hovered around him. The combination of the sound and smell and color made my stomach clutch.

"Is there some kind of alarm that makes this thing go off at midnight every time?" Luke said. "Damn, can't someone get a new refrigerator? What the fuck?"

Three things came to my mind then (four if you counted the thought *Luke is an asshole*), the three things that had been rat-scratching at the back of my brain since the first time the refrigerator banged, and not allowing my conscious mind to trap them.

Tatiana: "You may meet resistance."

The internet article: "All spirits may manifest through household appliances, creating shaking, bumping, hammering, and other auditory disturbances."

And this: I went back to my room, sat down at the computer, typed in GRANT MORRISON. Reread the article.

Grant Morrison, seventeen . . . was killed in a
hit-and-run incident this Saturday . . . at 12:03 a.m.

I HAD NO IDEA if there was a correlation between the banging refrigerator and Grant or if my exhausted, anxious mind had created one, but it certainly looked like the connection was real. I thought of Clark, laughing when I passed him the basketball, long limbs akimbo and the moose hat on his head. Tatiana had told us that she had been taken over by her mother, lost all that weight. Would anything be left of Clark at all if his dead brother took over his body forever?

It was time to send Grant back to wherever he came from.

I didn't even bother trying to talk to my mother; I

called Clark and woke him. "We have to go to Joshua Tree this weekend," I said.

THE WEEK SEEMED TO take forever. Clark and I followed our pattern of seeing each other only at school and staying busy with homework at night so we wouldn't tempt Grant to come. But no matter how much I read *Lady Chatterley's Lover* or studied for my math exam, nothing really distracted me from what I knew we were going to do when the weekend came.

Early Saturday morning I put on a hoodie, Doc Marten boots, and cutoffs over pink-and-black-striped tights, and packed a backpack with water, sunscreen, and PowerBars. I'd taken off work from Treasure Hunt in order to go on an "important family outing" as I'd called it. Mrs. Carol had happily obliged, asking me to keep an eye out for any good flea markets or garage sales; she seemed impressed with my fashion choices and how I dressed the mannequins in the windows.

"Where are you going?" my mom asked, shuffling into the kitchen in her bathrobe and slippers while I ate some toast. She blinked at the light and rubbed her eyes with her fists. "It's so early."

"Clark and I are going to the desert."

"Oh, sounds fun. I'm so glad you have each other," she said.

I wanted to say, *Yeah, so you don't feel as guilty about abandoning me*, but I kept my mouth shut. I didn't want to start an argument and hit the road too late.

"Well, I'm staying at Luke's tonight so don't worry if you get home and I'm not here," my mom said, kissing my cheek before going back to bed.

As if to punctuate her words, the refrigerator banged.

"Have fun," I growled at both of them.

RAINWATER

4

The light in the desert was different from the city, as Clark and I arrived there late that morning. Beautiful and clear, but *pitiless* was the word I thought of mostly, no shadows to soften things under the shimmering blue-white sky. The Joshua trees huddled watchfully along the road, their twisted arms pointing in different directions as if trying to confuse us.

Ed Rainwater's shop was on a ranch off the highway across from the Joshua Tree National monument. We drove up a dirt road and parked in front of the low sand-colored adobe building with a corral where a black stallion switched his tail at us.

Cactus and creosote grew by the front door. A sign read RAINWATER SAGE AND SWEAT. When we walked inside, we saw an extravagantly tall man in sunglasses, sitting on a stool behind a counter. At his side was a three-legged dog that resembled a coyote. Both of them shone with almost blinding white light in spite of the dimness of the room. The light was so strong that I wanted to ask Clark if he saw it. Especially the dog! Who knew dogs had auras like that?! I held my hand near Clark's face, so he would notice how the stone in my ring had brightened, but he didn't seem to see. He was preoccupied with the shop.

There were some cases full of polished stones and small figures carved out of bone, and intricate, feathered dream catchers hung from the ceiling. Bundles of dried sage covered the walls and I could smell the cleansing scent of the leaves smoldering in a small ceramic bowl. A German shepherd without ears and a pit bull with a scarred face were sleeping quietly on a worn brown leather couch.

"Are you Ed Rainwater?" I asked, and the tall man nodded. Then I introduced myself and Clark, and Ed shook our hands with his huge, calloused ones. They even made Clark's look small.

"What brings you here?" Ed Rainwater leaned forward and tilted up his sunglasses. I saw why he kept them on inside—not to scare away the customers; his eyes were fierce and full of so much feeling it was hard to meet their gaze for long.

"We need some sage," I said. "For a ritual."

Ed shook his head as he scattered tobacco onto a rolling paper. "What do you know about rituals?"

Neither of us said anything. We stood stiffly, side by side, not sure what to do next. Finally Clark said, "We're trying to learn, sir."

Ed rolled his cigarette slowly. His voice was gruff. "Looking for some kicks? Some native enlightenment?"

"No, sir," I said. "With all respect, we take this seriously. And even though I don't know anything about it, I'm half Cherokee." The words surprised me when I said them. I hoped they didn't sound disrespectful.

"Oh, really?"

"Yes, my father. He was full-blooded, supposedly. But I've never met him."

Ed looked at me, then at Clark, then back at me, then reached for a cowboy hat on the counter and set it over his black hair. He stood up, smoothing out his jeans along lengthy thighs, and picked up a bundle of the dried sage from the counter. "Come on."

I noticed a slight limp as he led us through the house to the back where desert plants—date palms and cactus—grew around a large cedar hot tub by a barbecue pit. The air smelled of charcoal and chlorine and a plant I knew was the fresh sagebrush. It had a pungent, head-clearing aroma that reminded me of the camphor my grandmother would rub on my chest when I had a cough.

Ed Rainwater knelt by the plant and picked off a leaf between his thumb and middle finger, holding it up for me to smell. My head felt instantly clear, almost as if I had jumped into a pool of water.

"This is what you want."

I took the leaf and held it carefully in my palm. The look on Ed's face, the whole gesture of his body as he handed it to me, told me this wasn't just any plant.

He gave us the bundle of dried sage he'd carried out with him. "We grow it special here. It's a rare form of *Salvia dorrii*. You light it when you're ready."

"What else do we do?" I asked. "If you don't mind . . . we're trying to release a spirit."

"See old Otto here?" he said. The German shepherd, who had followed us out, came over and put his head on Ed's bent knee. "They cut off his ears to make him a more aggressive fighter. What he went through should have killed him, but he didn't let it. Didn't let it kill his spirit. Most animals that are brutalized to that extent aren't redeemable, that's what people say. He came right into my arms when he saw me. The gentlest beast I've ever known."

"He's amazing," I said. "But I don't understand how this relates. I'm sorry, Mr. Rainwater, I don't want to be rude, it's just really frustrating."

"You'll understand when the time is right. No one can tell you. You have to find it in your own heart. Frightening as it may be."

So not helpful. I tried to explain, hoping it might make him change his mind. "I was trying to reach my grandma," I said. "But I haven't been able to. Clark's brother came instead. And it's getting really frightening, you're right. I need some kind of instruction or . . ."

Ed kicked at some dirt with the toe of his cowboy boot.

"You have to develop your skills."

"You mean because she can see colors and stuff?" Clark said.

"More than that. Your friend has a gift that can magnetize certain spirits." He wouldn't stop looking at me. I blinked hard and had to turn away.

"So Julie's a . . ." Clark started. "What do you call it? She has a spiritual gift?"

Ed nodded. "On her way to becoming. There are different terms."

I suppressed a nervous and inappropriate laugh, then hiccuped. "If that's true—and it just doesn't seem like I could be that, or have that, or whatever—but if it's true, what am I supposed to do with it? And by the way, I am so not ready."

Just then, a woman emerged from the building and we all turned and stared at her. I found it difficult to breathe. Metallic gold light was everywhere, even flickering in the ring on my finger. She had very long black hair, and skin that shone almost as much as the gold bracelets she wore. I couldn't tell how old she was. She smiled at me and extended a long hand that smelled mildly of cloves.

"I'm Amrita. Very nice to meet you." Her voice had a sweet, lightly sticky sound like honey made from orange blossoms, the *V* purred into a *W* sound. The dog Otto came and sat on top of her feet.

"Thank you," I said, still stunned at how gorgeous she was, like a Hindu goddess statue. I wouldn't have been surprised if she was hiding a few extra arms behind her back.

"We'll buy the sage," I said. "But we really need some more help." I looked at Amrita, trying to appeal to the goddess of compassion.

Ed and Amrita exchanged a glance. "You should stay for dinner," she said.

ED LIT A FIRE in the pit and we barbecued foil-wrapped fish and buttered vegetables on the coals. A light rain fell onto the protective awning, unleashing what Ed called the powerful medicine of the creosote that could clear the mind of all shadows. He told us that he had been a psychologist in Los Angeles but that he'd had to get away from the city.

"I had a practice there, but I can help people better when I'm not constantly fighting my environment," he said.

"So how did you come here?" Amrita asked us, stroking Otto's head.

I told them about Daiyu, Tatiana, and Florian, and the flyer in my grandmother's book. And I told them about the Ouija board and Grant.

Amrita's eyes had a faraway look as if she were watching a movie projected against the sky. "You have to prepare yourself."

As she spoke, clouds parted to reveal the sunset through the rain. We looked at the sky surrounding us on all sides and a rainbow appeared, as if painted in watercolor by a vast hand. It felt like some kind of a sign (from my grandmother?) and Ed and Amrita seemed to think so, too.

"The rainbow woman's come to visit," he said.

Amrita reached for his hand and nodded at him. He looked into her eyes and then leaned forward on his elbows and stirred the coals in the fire with a stick. Red sparks flew up, a kind of warning.

"I think your grandmother is with you," Amrita said. "Deep inside you, even if she's keeping quiet." She looked at Ed. "Tell them the other part."

He scowled at us and I shivered, pulling my sleeves down over my fingers. I had worn holes in most of my long-sleeved shirts from doing this so often. "You're dealing with another spirit, too. One who doesn't want to leave. We can help you by doing a sweat and some meditation techniques."

Meditation? The idea of sitting still like that made me anxious just to think of it. Amrita noticed and stroked her long braid as she spoke. "It can be learned. It's to calm the mind in the face of chaos and ultimately prepare us for our transition to the next realm. You may need it for something else, I'm guessing. A vibrational protection."

"A vibrator protector?" Clark said. He seemed to make especially bad jokes when he was anxious. I whacked his arm. Amrita ignored us and went on. "You *conceive* that your cells are vibrating very fast, much faster than anything that is trying to invade your energy body. It creates a barrier."

I felt a drafty sensation in my chest as if it were a hollow cavern through which cold wind blew.

She must have seen the concern in my eyes. "It'll be a bit of a crash course, but I have a feeling you'll be a quick study."

I didn't want to do this. Sitting and breathing was the last thing I wanted to do. I wanted to go home and try to reach my grandma, but I didn't know how to say no to this goddess. She was already walking away, across the yard to a small patio. I followed her like a reluctant but obedient puppy while Clark stayed with Ed.

"Sit down, cross-legged," she said.

I did so. Light rain fell through the branches of the tree

that overhung the patio.

"Breathe through your nose with your mouth closed, making a whispery sound like you're taking in air through a hole in your throat."

I found the image disturbing—like a tracheotomy—and frowned at her but she ignored me.

"Fill every cell with breath," she went on. "Imagine yourself surrounded by a body of rose-colored light. And that your cells are dancing particles of light, dancing very fast."

The whole idea sounded weird and too hard to do anyway. At first my mind kept drifting—did I look like an idiot? When could we leave?—but after a while a tingling sensation spread across the surface of my skin, warming me in spite of the rain. Listening to Amrita's honey voice, I could imagine my cells dancing faster and faster.

"This is what I mean by the vibrational protection," she said softly, but it startled me.

And I lost my breath.

What did I need to protect myself from? Grant's face appeared in my mind; the whites of his eyes were red. My own eyes flicked open and I gasped for air.

"I can't," I said. "I can't sit still like this."

Amrita took a bottle of oil from her pocket and touched a drop to her finger. The lavender fragrance reminded me of Grandma Miriam and calmed me immediately.

"May I?" she asked.

I let her touch a drop of lavender oil to each of my temples. "Keep practicing. All this is necessary."

"How do I do it at home?" I couldn't even sit peacefully here, let alone in my musty room with the sounds of heavy metal music and evil refrigerators shaking the walls.

"Set up a special altar with some candles, a white one for healing, a red for knowledge, green to attract luck, maybe an object or two that is important to you. Try five minutes at a time at first and work up to an hour. Focus on your breath, just the way I showed you. It will help you handle what's to come."

"What if I start thinking about other stuff?"

"You will. Just bring it back to the breath," she said. I scowled and she smiled at me, surprisingly feral teeth between gentle-looking lips. "I know, it's easier said than done. Our thoughts are wild creatures who've been wounded countless times. We have to tame them."

LATER CLARK AND I, wearing the over-sized cotton promotional (RAINWATER SAGE AND SWEAT) T-shirts we'd been given, stood with Ed and Amrita at the entrance to a low building; we had to crouch to enter. Inside rocks were piled on the coals, and Ed poured water to make them steam. I was hot right away and soon beads of sweat were popping out of every pore. It was hard to find air and I had to concentrate on my breath in order not to panic and pass out. A couple of times I almost crawled for the entrance. Clark sat bolt upright across from me, eyes closed, sweat trickling down his face. Ed mumbled something I did not understand. But it had the rhythm of prayer and his voice was so resonant I could feel the words penetrating my skin.

He turned to me then, and spoke clearly.

"What do you want to release?"

"Grief," I said.

Ed nodded. I couldn't see his face clearly, but I knew the fierceness I'd have seen in his black eyes if I could.

"And you." He turned to Clark. It was a question but spoken as a statement.

Clark said, "Fear? At least that's what all these random strangers keep telling me. And . . . I can't . . ."

Ed said, "Try."

Clark wasn't joking around now. His voice was deeper when he spoke. "Fear. And my brother. But I'm not ready yet."

"Thank you for your honesty," said Ed Rainwater. "He's not ready either. It may be hard work. This will help but it's not enough. It will have to come from you."

Great. These healers looked impressive but they all pretty much said the same unhelpful things. I knew Clark was sharing my thought by the way he raised his eyebrows in my direction.

When the sweat was over, he and I had to hold on to each other to get outside; our legs were weak. But as we stood in the rain, I felt the drops slide down my skin and it was as if everything that had been released from my body was washed away. I raised my hands over my head and spun around slowly, not worrying about the size of my bare thighs. For the first time since I was a small child, I felt graceful in my body and at ease in my skin. There was a painful but pleasant lump in my throat as I looked at Clark standing there in the wet dark, his eyes familiar and yet lost. No awkwardness between us, maybe for the first time. I wanted to stay here with him forever and forget everything in Los Angeles. We had been sent out into the world for something and I wondered if what we had been sent for was this moment and nothing more.

Amrita handed us towels. "Ed tells me you have some Native American blood," she said softly, stroking my wet hair the way my mom did and I suddenly missed her.

"My dad was. But he was a surrogate so I don't know much about him."

"Cherokee, right? Like Ed," Amrita said. There was a curious look on her face as she glanced back and forth between Ed Rainwater and me. "How did you find us, again?"

"My grandma had an advertisement for your store in

her book. I just found it and it mentioned the sage. We figured we should come."

Ed nodded and looked at me, hard. "The meditation will help you. And pay attention to your dreams, especially the difficult ones."

"I only get little bits that don't make sense."

"Keep trying to remember and you'll have more."

I wasn't sure I wanted to. And none of this provided an answer to the question that brought us here in the first place. "What about the ritual?" I asked. "What are we supposed to do?"

"It's always different, depending on the person who performs it, depending on the spirit. You must be creative and find your own. It's an art, it takes practice.

"Now get back home," said Ed. "You have work to do. And not much time."

Not much time? Before I could say anything more, Ed and Amrita had turned away and were walking back into the shop, holding hands, the top of her head barely reaching his shoulder, Otto waiting at the door for them.

"MAN," CLARK SAID IN the car on the way home. "All these healers are like something out of *Buffy*. Central casting central." He was trying to make light of it, but I knew he was shaken. Not that either of us ever *weren't* feeling that way lately. "And this whole thing about, 'We can't help you. It has to come from you. Do it yourself.' They should be on Etsy."

This actually made me laugh and Clark smiled at me sideways; I could tell he was proud of his joke.

The desert sped by; Joshua trees surrounding us on all sides for miles witnessed our departure. My body was empty and weak from the sweat, from the whole day. I propped my head in my hand, leaned against the window, and shut my eyes.

I WOKE JAMMING MY foot against the floorboards again and again.

"What's wrong? Julie!" Clark shouted.

I looked at him gripping the steering wheel, then ahead at the car eating the white lines on the dark road and I opened the window for air but I couldn't speak yet, not with my stomach way up in my throat.

"What happened?" Clark said, softer now.

"I had a dream. A car accident." I couldn't remember the details; only that it felt real enough to slam through my body. Slam my foot on an imaginary brake. Was it another dream about Grant?

"Damn, dude, you scared the crap out of me," said Clark. "Are you okay?"

I nodded and leaned my head out the window, into the

wind, remembering Ed's words, wondering if I was going to have to remember more dreams like this one.

IT WAS ALMOST DAWN when Clark dropped me off. I hadn't bothered to call my mom, mostly because I was still mad at her from Thanksgiving and my birthday. I figured that she didn't care what I was doing anyway. She hardly ever questioned me about where I was going or when I'd be home. Though she had said it was because she trusted me and Clark, I thought it had to do with the fact that she was too busy thinking about Luke. I just hoped he wasn't at the apartment.

When I saw that her car was there but not Luke's truck, I felt the anxiety-bubble in my chest deflate. Until I got inside.

The light on the answering machine was blinking the number twelve.

No one called us that much.

And my mom wasn't home.

I scrambled in my bag for my phone, remembering I'd forgotten to turn it back on. There were ten new messages there as well.

The balloon of anxiety was now ready to burst me open. I checked the last text I'd received.

There's been an accident. Call immediately. Luke.

PART III

Is as it had not been—

THE VISITOR

1

After I spoke to Luke, I called Clark crying, but it was Grant who pulled up in the same car that had taken us to the desert, his face and voice rough with sleeplessness, although perhaps he had been asleep while Clark was awake and now the reverse was true. (It made my brain feel like an overstuffed stomach to think about this.) I recognized the dead twin immediately.

"Why are you here?" I said.

"Because you need me. I'm better than he is during crisis."

I knew I didn't have time to waste so I got in the car with a ghost anyway. "She's at Cedars Sinai."

We drove in silence for a while. My arms were crossed over my chest as I tried to keep myself from rocking back and forth in the seat like a straitjacketed mental patient.

"Do you want to know where I've been?" he asked.

"Not really."

He ignored this. "I've been giving you your space. And him. To let you realize that you need me."

"He needs you to leave," I said, gripping the door handle as Grant raced through a yellow light that was turning red, thinking, in spite of myself, that Clark, even in an emergency, would have stopped cautiously instead.

Grant looked at me sideways. "But what about you?" he asked softly, his voice deeper than usual. The traffic lights played off his cheekbones. His dilated pupils made his eyes look black. Even in my fear, or maybe in part because of it, I felt desire for him queasy in my belly and tense between my legs.

THE AIR WAS FREEZING when we stepped into the hospital lobby, so cold I was surprised I couldn't see my breath. I felt myself grow numb under the sick-making fluorescent lights. If I stopped experiencing any sensations in my body, I might be able to escape it and the world, get away. I was glad to have someone at the hospital with me, even though he was dead.

My mom was in the ER with a broken leg and a concussion, and Luke, who'd been pretty unscathed in the car accident, had gone home by the time we got there. Luke was driving. They'd been coming home from a bar.

She was so out of it that I was worried she wouldn't know who I was, but she kept saying, "I'm so sorry I wasn't with you at Thanksgiving!"

"It's okay, Mom." I stroked her head.

"Are you going to drive her home?" the nurse said.

I looked at Grant, who nodded. I wondered what she would think if she knew who he was. It didn't really matter; there weren't funds for more than one day in the hospital, even if the person who took you home had been killed in a car crash once.

The air smelled of fire as we drove south toward the apartment. It smelled of fire and of fear, a deep belly terror, the kind that could turn you inside out.

Grant and I helped my mother inside. She gripped my arm, digging her fingernails in.

She kept asking, "Where's Luke? Where's Luke?"

I told her he was okay and had gone home to sleep, but I had the same question. Where was he? Why wasn't he taking care of her? How had he let this happen?

We got her inside, in bed. Gave her more pain pills and something to help her sleep.

Grant took my hand and led me to the kitchen. My limbs felt dead as I stumbled after him.

"You have to eat." He opened the refrigerator and brought out a container of black-rice-and-currant *kicharee* with cinnamon Clark had sent home with me from school on Friday.

"I can't," I said.

He opened the container, sniffed it, and rolled his eyes. "I don't blame you. I want a hamburger, myself. Make that a double cheeseburger. With fries. Strawberry milk shake."

Even though my mouth was suddenly watering for sugar and fried grease instead of *kicharee,* it also made me nauseous to think about and I missed Clark then, with a bang in my chest as forceful as the refrigerator at 12:03. How had I allowed this to happen, to accept Grant again? My eyes felt like pebbles; I was so tired. When was the last time I'd slept? It seemed like a week had passed since we'd left for the desert.

Grant put the *kicharee* back in the refrigerator. "Come with me to get some food."

"What's this thing you're doing with the banging at midnight?" I said, ignoring him.

"Well, no one's banging me at midnight."

I glared at him.

"Sorry, not funny."

"Not at all," I said. My anger had brought me back to myself a bit. "You like hanging out inside the refrigerator when you're not possessing your brother's body?"

"Not exactly. I don't *hang out* there. I'm just trying to get your attention. Since you started snooping around town talking to all these psychics. 'He's going to take over and pretty soon there won't be anything left of you.' 'Angry ghost.' '*Espíritu maligno.*' "

He was looking down at me, smirking, but then his expression changed, softened, and for a second I thought I saw Clark flicker in him.

"It's like he's dead when you do that," I said. "Where does he even go?" I couldn't control the escalating pitch of my voice. "Are you willing to basically kill your brother so that you can stay?"

"Listen, Julie. I love Clark, but I don't have a choice about this and neither do you."

"What do you mean, neither do I?"

Grant leaned close to me so that I could feel the heat coming off his skin. I now realized how weird this was considering his true chill. I could also smell him, a scent weirdly different from Clark's—spicier, denser. "You need me. Who else will help you with your mom? With your grandma?"

I backed away and bumped into the kitchen counter. "I need a human."

Grant's jaw clenched; he spun and pounded his fist on the refrigerator door. "I am so fucking sick of this," he said.

"And of you and my brother with your little rituals to try to what? Send me to hell? I'm going to get sent back anyway, Julie. On the anniversary of my death, which is coming right up. Unless I send him there first."

My hands reflexively went up to my chest, warding him off.

"Sweetie?" my mom called. "What's going on?"

"It's okay," I managed. *He can't go near her.*

I kept my eyes on Grant as I backed out of the room. "Please leave now," I said.

My mom was trying to move around, tugging at the sheets. The hair on her forehead was damp with sweat, loose strands sticking to her face. "I don't know what happened," she said. "I'm sorry."

I stroked her forehead and tried to remember to breathe the way Amrita had taught me. To keep away the invaders, the danger. Grant was the danger, but somehow I had forgotten. Why had I let him go with me to the hospital at all?

When I went back into the kitchen, Grant was gone.

Relief coursed through me, washing away everything except the need to sleep.

I WOKE THE NEXT evening; the sky was darkening among the palm trees. My body felt heavy and hot. What had happened? What day was it? Where was my mom? Where was

Clark? Had Grant been here?

Clark and I were in Joshua Tree. Grant and I were at the hospital. They had both left in one body. Grant had said something about sending Clark to hell.

And I'd had another strange dream. It had nothing to do with Clark or Grant. Instead I had dreamed randomly of Ally Kellogg. I was walking around naked at her Halloween party. The stone lions had come to life and were roaming the rooms. Ms. Merritt was there, with a tall, thin man in black whose face I couldn't see, and she didn't seem to recognize me when I approached her. The claw-foot table was doing the rumba. Monsters were having sex with each other on the floor, leaving trails of organs in their wake. None of this seemed to bother me particularly. Until I went outside and saw Jason Weitzman pissing into the pool, which was filled with bloody appendages.

"Where's Ally?" I asked him.

He turned to look at me, pointing his finger into the pool, and I woke up.

My mom was calling for me so I dragged myself out of bed and stumbled into her room, my body still buzzing from the dream.

She reached out for me and I went into her arms, but it didn't feel safe there, not the way I wanted it to. And I saw the gray color coming off her like it had the day she lost her job.

I still didn't know exactly what it meant or why I was able to see auras at all, but I knew the gray wasn't a good sign.

"I'm sorry," she said again, more lucid now.

"It's okay, Mom. What happened? Was he drinking? I'll kill him if he was drinking." Luke hadn't sounded wasted on the phone, but I wasn't sure. I turned Tatiana's ring on my finger, remembering the bile-green color I'd seen on Luke and in the ring the night I called Clark to say we were going to Joshua Tree. Had the color been a warning that I had ignored? Could I have helped my mother if I'd known how to interpret it? Were there other signs I'd been ignoring?

"He wasn't drinking. But we got in a fight."

"About what?"

"He just doesn't seem like he's serious about us. Maybe because I'm older. Or broke. Or depressed."

I wanted to take her by the shoulders and shake her, even in her broken state. "Why do you even see him?"

She put her face in her hands. "When Grandma died . . . I didn't realize how much it would hurt to not have her around. It was like I lost my whole sense of who I was. Like I was a little kid again without her. And then he came right away and comforted me. I couldn't ask you to do it and I didn't have anyone else. She was the one who had always comforted me. The only reason I was able to have you by myself, without the support of a man, was because I had her.

Other women can do it, but I couldn't."

She started to cry and I sat very still, feeling the heat of her body, the wet of her tears on my face. Part of me wanted to dissolve into her and part of me wanted to run away, but I said, "It's okay. I understand."

I thought of Grant. How he had made me believe I was special, how I had allowed him to kiss me. How vulnerable I still was. At least Luke was alive. I never wanted to have to depend on someone like that again, especially not someone who didn't deserve my trust.

"I just miss you. I'm scared. I feel really alone," I sputtered. "It's like you're not here."

"I guess I wasn't. I wasn't sure I could live without my mommy." She closed her eyes and leaned back against the pillows.

"I can't," I said.

"You won't have to anymore," she mumbled.

But it wasn't true. When I started to tell her about my nightmare, she was already asleep again.

I went into my room and sat cross-legged on the floor, trying to clear my mind and focus on breathing the way Amrita had taught me, but I was assaulted with images from the hospital, the dream about Ally, and especially Grant standing in my kitchen, telling me and Clark to go to hell.

～つ

BEFORE SCHOOL THE NEXT day, I found Ally Kellogg applying lip gloss in the mirror she'd attached to the inside of her locker.

"Hi, Ally. Can I talk to you?" I was trying to hide the urgency beating in my throat.

She gave me a disinterested smile. "Sure. What's up, Julie?"

"I'm sorry," I said. "I feel weird about this, but I had a dream about you."

She turned from the mirror and frowned at me. It was odd to see a crease in her smooth face. "Uh-huh."

"I mean, the dream doesn't matter, it's just that . . ."

"I have to get to class," she said, not unpleasantly but without her usual smile.

"Wait, I'm sorry, it's just that I was kind of freaked out by this dream. And I thought I should tell you. Because I think sometimes dreams can mean something or . . . that you should listen to them."

She waited, tapping her fingernails on her locker. I noticed little decals of different flowers on each finger.

"I just think you should be careful around Jason Weitzman," I said softly.

"Around who?"

"Jason Weitzman."

"Okay. Yeah, sure. I'll be careful. Thanks, Julie." She

was watching me with narrowed eyes and I realized I had made a mistake in telling her. But I was worried about her safety after the dream. I was worried about everything, it seemed. My mom, Grant, and Clark.

When I saw him in math, he just said, "Hey," and I realized that he didn't know anything about the accident. Evidently it was Grant, not Clark who had answered the phone when I called, but I'd been crying so hard that I hadn't noticed. I told him that my mom and Luke had been in a crash but they were okay.

"Why didn't you call me?" he asked when the bell rang and we left the room.

I almost whispered my answer. "I did."

There was a silence between us that stretched for the length of the entire hallway.

"It happened again," he said.

"Yes."

"Can I come over after school?" he asked in a voice that was deep with tension, but still his voice, not his brother's.

"I think you better."

"It's really time, isn't it?"

"Yes," I said.

THAT EVENING, WHEN MY mom was aslccp, I got out thc tincture and gem essence from the cabinet but when I opened the refrigerator for the rosewater I put my hand over my face; the stench was like rotting meat even though the fridge was empty and clean.

"What is that smell?" Clark asked when he got there, handing me a pot of chestnut, wild rice, and cranberry *kicharee* he'd brought.

"It's been here ever since we first went to Daiyu," I said. "Ever since we got the essences."

Clark grasped a dry sliver of cuticle between his teeth and pulled.

And then I realized . . .

"He started it when he knew we were planning to get rid of him," I said. "He's pissed."

"Shit. I guess it is time."

"But he said he'd have to go back anyway, on the anniversary of his death," I said.

"What is that supposed to mean?"

"I have no idea. He said he'd have to go back where he came from unless you went instead."

Clark continued to gnaw on his fingers. "Go where? This is getting more f-ed up all the time."

We stood staring at each other, not moving. But the smell from the refrigerator was so foul I had to cover my mouth again.

"Come on," I said.

We went into my room, away from the smell, and I sprayed Clark and then myself heavily with the rosewater—it was spicy rather than sweet, yet very delicate, and felt both warm and cool at the same time. For sustenance we ate the *kicharee*, and for strength from fear and grief we dropped the tinctures into our mouths and applied the essences to the insides of our wrists. When we were done, we lit a circle of white candles and set the sage on fire in the flames, moving the bundles in circles with our arms as we faced each direction so that the smoke surrounded us.

Then we sat on the floor with the Ouija board, dried mugwort scattered over its surface. I took a series of deep breaths to clear my mind and calm my body and concentrated on my cells vibrating rapidly, as Amrita had taught me, too fast for anything to penetrate them.

"Grandma, please help us," I said. "Please tell me what we're supposed to do."

Clark nodded soberly, his mouth pressed closed so that the skin around his lips looked white.

The marker began to move almost immediately, gliding toward the *G* on the board. But before any more letters were revealed the marker careened across the surface, arcing back and forth as we tried to keep our fingers on it, until it slid off and onto the floor. The candles flickered and went out and I heard the bang of the refrigerator and smelled the rot even in my room, as if it had permeated my nostrils. I tried to get up but I was dizzy, and my legs were so weak they couldn't hold me. I took the rosewater and sprayed the air around us again; my hands were shaking as I tried to light the candles and the match went out. Clark took the matches from me and struck one, lit one candle, and cupped his hand around it to protect the flame, but it flared, sputtered, and went out again. He threw down the matches and sat on the bed.

"Fuck! I don't want him to go. No wonder it's not working. I don't even want him to go."

I managed to get up and sit next to him in the dark room. "I know," I said. "But I think we have to do it now."

"We go to all these people, all these wise healer shamans or whatever they are, and they don't tell us anything. Except we have to find it inside ourselves. I can't find anything inside myself. I'm more empty than he is. Emptiness and fucking devastation, she said. It's better when he just takes over. I'd rather he just do it and replace me." He was breathing hard, pulling at his hair. I wanted to make him stay still.

"Don't say that."

"It's true, though. He was the one that should have lived." Clark got up and jammed his fedora onto his head. "I have to leave," he said.

He stopped at the door. "My parents are going to San

Francisco over winter break. I wasn't going to go, but I think I better now. I need to get away. We'll be back on Christmas Eve."

"Please, Clark," I said. "I don't think it's safe. He said things about you. He was really angry."

Clark shook his head and wouldn't look at me. He turned and left, closing the door behind him with a sound that resonated throughout the apartment. I realized there was nothing more I could say to keep him from leaving, nothing I could do to protect him or anyone else. The grief and fear I'd been trying so hard to ward off flooded me like an icy wave crashing into an empty cove.

CLARK TEXTED ME TO say he wasn't coming to school the next day; he wasn't feeling well. When I texted him back, he didn't respond.

There was a cluster of kids around my locker when I got there before school. Someone had written *Psycho Bitch* on it, in red Sharpie. My face was probably the same color as I hurried away. I hoped that Ally Kellogg hadn't told Jason what I'd said, as much for her sake as my own, but it was probably too late.

After English, I asked Ms. Merritt if I could speak to her. I really wanted to tell her the whole story, but I knew I couldn't.

"Is everything okay, Julie?" she asked in that kind voice

that always made me feel like crying.

"Yeah, it's fine." I couldn't tell her.

"How's your report coming?"

"I want to do it on Dickinson, but I'm a little scared to," I said.

"Why?" she asked. "You know I love her work. Obviously." She made a sweeping gesture of her body, from bun to brown dress to sensible heels, and laughed.

"It's kind of emotional for me, to be honest. My grandma loved her poetry and I'm afraid it will bring up too much for me to look at it that closely."

I'd written about my grandma in my essay, so Ms. Merritt knew she had died. I'd never noticed how much even my teacher's wide-set brown eyes were like the poet's, in that one uncanny photo.

"I understand. But sometimes that's the best way to deal with things like that. It might help you feel closer to her. Maybe I'm not the most objective source, but poetry can sometimes have the answers. I think you should definitely do your report on Emily Dickinson, Julie."

It was hard to say no to my grandmother's favorite poet's doppelganger.

Mrs. Carol was closing the store for two weeks to visit her daughter up north, so I had more time to take care of my mom during winter break. I stayed in the apartment watching movies with her and making soup, only going out for groceries. It was Hanukkah, but without my grandmother, we didn't feel like doing anything. I didn't even buy candles for the menorah.

My mom didn't return Luke's daily calls, the refrigerator didn't bang. I worked on my Emily Dickinson project. It was going to be about death in her poems, but I hadn't quite figured out what to focus on. I did the eye exercises from Tatiana's book on how to read auras and took my herbal tincture and applied the gem essences and set up an altar as Amrita had instructed. I tried to breathe deeply and meditate. But sitting still for even a few minutes when I wasn't about to go to sleep made me wired with anxiety, as if I'd explode from the heat in my circuitry. Still, I continued to try.

Whenever I got really anxious I texted Clark. He texted me back but not as promptly as he used to, and I remembered the cold wave crashing in my belly the last night I'd seen him. I wondered if he'd still want to see me when he came back.

I took the jade urn of ashes into my room every night, and lay on my bed and talked to my grandmother, asking her to come to me in my dreams.

I didn't see her. I saw the car, a bright red car, speeding around sharp curves. I couldn't make out the driver's face but I knew who he was. Smelled like formaldehyde and rotten meat, made your stomach heave up into your throat. Called Grim by some, called Reaper, called Azrael, Thanatos. If you Googled slang words you'd find hundreds, from A through Z, Adiosland to Zombie Factory. Emily Dickinson had many names, including "Visitor." In a lot of her poems she even sounded like she was in love with him, like she *wanted* him to take her away.

Was that what I wanted, too? Was Grant the driver of the car? Was it the red Honda he'd died in?

When I woke up, I wrote down the dream. I knew what I was going to write my report on: Death. As the Lover.

ALTHOUGH WE DIDN'T CELEBRATE Christmas, my grandmother always did something special like order really good Chinese food and make cookies and then we'd go see a movie— usually one of the big fantasy films that came out around that time of year. That Christmas Eve, I took two separate pints of Ben and Jerry's ice cream out of the freezer and put in Fellini's *Juliet of the Spirits* for me and my mom to watch. She'd named me after the main character, who is haunted by ghosts, though I knew my mother had no idea how accurate that would prove to be. She opened a bottle of wine and had a couple of glasses. I shouldn't have let her.

When the phone rang, she answered it. I knew right

away who it was by the nervous, light sound of her voice and the way she wouldn't look at me.

"Can you excuse me for a second, honey?" she said, not meeting my eyes.

She couldn't get up easily because of her cast. I wanted to tell her no, I couldn't excuse her, there were no excuses for what she was doing, but I got up and went to my room and slammed the door instead. She knocked a few minutes later and told me Luke wanted to come by with some presents. I didn't answer her.

Before I went to bed I texted Clark.

He didn't respond. Was he still angry about what happened?

I fell asleep almost right away and woke to the sound of something hitting against my window. Pebbles? Really? Were we in some kind of a tween movie? I got up and looked outside and saw a hatless boy standing in the street. The Christmas lights made everything except his dark figure glow with a soft silver haze like he was the only thing real in a ghost world.

"Hey, Julie," he said. "I'm sorry about what I said. I was just so scared. Can I come talk to you?"

I looked at the urn of ashes that I'd kept by my bed from the night before. Where was my grandmother? I felt as if I was a walking sack of ash myself. "Devastation and emptiness," Daiyu had said. That wasn't just Grant; that was me. Even Emily Dickinson allowed Death to court her.

I let him in.

My mother and Luke were in her room; I could hear him playing a CD of his band The Descent. I still hadn't gotten used to my mom as a heavy metal fan.

Luke's music throbbed through the walls. My mom was "gone" again.

Clark had not responded to my text. Grant had come.

Grant and I hardly spoke; for once we both wanted the same thing.

We sat on the bed. I needed him to knock me out like a sleeping pill, like a pain pill, kill me with sensation until I didn't feel anything. Without a word, he fixed his lips to mine, slid his tongue into my mouth, and I was comforted by the warm rhythm, like music. He stroked my throat and I tingled, the delicate flesh parts of my body rising toward him. Then he reached his hand gently across my belly, slid it up between my ribs, between my breasts. I was sweating.

"Is this okay?" he asked.

"You mean because you are possessing Clark's body or because you are touching me?"

"The touching part."

"That part is more okay," I said, tugging at the hem of his T-shirt.

"I don't want to make things harder for you," he said. "But I don't want to go."

He put his arms around me and pulled me so close, I could feel how our bodies fit together if we were lying horizontally. I was trembling and he held me against him like he was trying to make the tremors stop.

"Just be with me once," he said. "I never had the chance." He was really crying, not trying to hide it. My heart felt like a piece of raw meat. What about Clark?

I might have said his name out loud because Grant said, "He'll understand. I think he will understand. I'd do the same for him if it were the reverse."

He ran his fingers lightly over my breast, lingering on the nipple that flicked up to meet him in spite of the fact that he was a spirit inside his brother. He pulled my shirt up and put his mouth there. My body dissolved beneath him, nothing left of me but that spot of sensation where he was. Until he pushed his other hand between my thighs, pressing so that the seam of my jeans dug gently into me, in exactly the right spot. I writhed against him and he left my breast and came back up to my mouth, falling on top of me in a kiss that included every part of both our still-clothed bodies.

"I am so fucking done with being dead," he said. "Thank God for you, baby."

No boy had called me baby. No boy had ever thanked

God for me. I hadn't really cared, before, if any boy did. Now I cared.

I helped him pull his T-shirt over his head. His chest looked slender but stronger than I'd expected, and his skin was very smooth and so warm. I clenched around his thigh. We were both breathing in this raspy way so I couldn't tell who was who. I wanted him to push his way inside me and for him to come alive like that, or for me to be dead. I didn't care which, just some transformation, terrible and profound, a ghost brought back, a girl taken away. Sweat dripped off his brow onto my face. I thought of Clark, his silly smile, his hats, his *kicharee*. I loved him. But he was here, too, in a way. Wasn't he? The aching in my body was speaking louder than my heart, justifying what it wanted me to do. My hands skimmed Grant's hips and I felt something in his pocket.

"What's this?" I whispered, sliding out a crunchy condom packet.

"Are you ready?" he asked me. "Is it okay?"

Then I remembered my mom in the other room. With Luke. Probably doing this same thing. To heavy metal.

She and I with our dead men, trying to be dead, too.

We were exactly the same.

I started to cry and Grant stopped moving above me.

"What?" he said. His voice was harsh now.

"Clark!" I called. "Clark."

Then the boy above me reached for the flashlight I kept by the bed for emergencies and shone it in my face. Moons of hot light blinded me until my eyes adjusted and I saw him. Clark.

In the kitchen, the refrigerator sounded like someone was pummeling it from inside. Something big and cold and mad.

Clark looked down at me, moved away. "How did I get here? Fuck."

I pulled my shirt back over my chest. I couldn't speak.

"What happened?"

"Clark . . ."

He shone the flashlight around the room and saw the condom wrapper on the floor. Looked down at his own bare chest. "He tried to have sex with you?"

I nodded.

"Did you want to? Julie?"

I couldn't look at him. I thought of Grant trying to get me to look into his eyes the first time I went to Clark's house and that was difficult, but for a different reason. Now I was guilty.

He shook his head like a big, sad dog and ducked into his T-shirt.

"I called for you," I said, dreading the sound of the door closing behind my best friend, even though I knew I didn't deserve to have him stay.

"I think I should go. Will you be okay tonight?" He started for the door before I could answer.

"Clark?" I said.

He froze with his back to me. "What?"

I wanted to say I was sorry, but the words wouldn't come. And they felt inadequate anyway after what I'd done. Instead I said, "Never mind."

IT WAS NEW YEAR'S Eve. My mom, in her cast and a little black dress, and on crutches, was out with Luke, probably listening to some metal bands.

The guilt she'd felt about the date was apparent; before she left, she'd barraged me with questions: "Are you going to see Clark? Why haven't you seen him? Are you in a fight or something? Are any of your other friends having parties?"

Other friends? Right. The truth was, I never felt like going to another party for the rest of my life even if I *had* any friends besides Clark. And that friendship was on tenterhooks.

I didn't answer my mother. I'd hardly spoken to her for a week although she kept begging me to forgive her and promising that Luke wasn't going to drink when they went out, that he'd drive safely. Whatever.

I drank some leftover wine in the fridge to wipe me out as much as possible and went to bed early.

When I woke, I lay on my back, staring at the stucco ceiling, trying to catch my breath. The red digital numbers told me it was 11:45. My head ticked with pain like a demonic clock.

I had dreamed of the red car again and I felt the now-familiar queasy bubbling in my stomach that followed it. I wrote the dream down so I would remember it, as Ed had suggested, but it felt insignificant, just another distraction.

I still hadn't dreamed of my grandma like I wanted, but everything that had happened in the last six months felt like a dream. My grandmother dying in my arms. A Ouija board. A dead twin. A possession. A searching. White candles, mugwort, roses, sage. An accident. A quaking appliance. A hellish stench. All I wanted was for my grandmother to help me understand what had happened. She was so far away. All that was left were ashes, some photos and jewelry and dresses and purses, poetry books, a bottle of perfume. Why had she left me without teaching me how to reach her? Why had she waited until the last second, when it was too late? She hadn't known when she was going to die but she knew that eventually she would. Maybe, she was worried she'd upset me if she brought it up.

I got out of bed and it almost felt as if I were watching my body move across the room. I dropped some of Daiyu's tincture into my mouth and touched the lavender oil and

Shalimar to my wrists.

"Let's try now," I said to my grandma, Miriam.

I pulled the photo album from under my bed and put it on the floor next to the urn and surrounded them both with a circle of white votives, which I lit, one by one. I sat down with my legs crossed, closed my eyes, and began to breathe with the Ouija board balanced on my knees, my fingers on the marker.

"Grandma?"

Trying not to think of anything in particular, I took a series of deep breaths through my nose, making the whispery sound at the base of my throat. Visions flitted across the dark space behind my eyes—my grandmother standing in front of me, holding the book of Emily Dickinson's poetry open in her hands, my mother getting into Luke's car, Clark in a hotel room, staring out the window at a city enshrouded in fog. I tried to acknowledge each image and then let it go.

Grant's face appeared in my mind then. This image would not be so easily breathed away. As if I needed it. As if I needed him to help me.

"I can help you reach her," a voice said.

I opened my eyes with a bang in my chest. Grant was sitting there quietly, watching.

"What the hell? How did you get in?"

You called him, Julie.

"I'm pretty agile," he said calmly.

"Get out," I told him. "You scared the shit out of me. You can't just come in like that. Get out!"

"I've come to help you with your grandmother."

"Why would you do that?" He had mentioned Clark and my "little rituals." Grant had started playing tricks with the refrigerator after Clark and I began to consider sending him away. The dead brother must have known that we were trying to reach Grandma Miriam in order to get rid of him, so why would he want to help me now?

"Because she'll understand. She'll know how to help us all."

I could feel my eyes narrowing at him, my jaw tightening. "What do you know about her?"

Grant moved closer. "You still have her ashes. You need to scatter them. Then you'll reach her."

"How do you know?"

"I'm dead, remember? I know about it. My family just tried to move away and forget me, repress the whole thing. See what happens with that? I won't take off." He smiled but his mouth made a hard line. "Let's scatter her ashes."

"My mom isn't ready."

"She doesn't have to be ready. She doesn't have to know. You can scatter them and put in some fake ones. She'll never know. She's never going to touch them anyway. She's scared."

In my head I heard what sounded like glass breaking. "Stop it. I'm not ready."

"Don't you see? You want your grandmother to be close to you, but you are holding on too tight."

"I'm not," I stammered. I wasn't holding on to my grandmother's life but lately, more and more, I was holding on to her death. I wanted to hover in a netherworld bathed in her ashes, I wanted to live inside that jade urn with her. The fact that I had allowed Grant to get so close to me was just more proof that I wanted to cling to death and not let go.

"Come with me," said he, my ghost of devastation and emptiness. "To scatter them."

WE DROVE ALONG PACIFIC Coast Highway with the windows down and the cool breeze tasting of gasoline and salt on my lips. I was holding the heavy, light-green urn on my lap.

I didn't want to let her go. It wasn't the time. It hadn't been a year yet, and my mother wasn't with me. My grandma would have wanted to be scattered nearer to where Maury was.

But maybe Grant was right and it didn't seem as if I had time to waste. He knew something about the spirit world that I didn't.

We parked, took off our shoes, rolled up our jeans, and went down to the water. The sand was cold and my feet sunk in; it was hard to move forward. The water was shining and black. *Black jade,* I thought. I wanted to go into that dark, wet, vast space with her, part of me did. My life was cramped into a little box with a mother who didn't know she was as much in love with death as I was, an urn full of ashes to talk to, a friend who was so wounded that he no longer cared if he stayed, conscious, in the world. All I had now was Grant, a ghost. A ghost I wanted to go with, one I would follow anywhere, it seemed.

We waded out onto the rocks, the urn balanced on my hip. You weren't legally allowed to scatter ashes there, but he said no one would know and I let myself believe him. As we climbed up onto a large rock, the soles of my feet snagged on the jagged surface. I gripped his arm for balance. The waves sloshed at our feet, dragging at us, dragging us in if they could. I opened the top of the urn and reached inside, cringing. The ashes felt soft, with a few hard particles. Grant was beside me, facing the churning, wet darkness, his eyes closed and a small smile on his face, one I couldn't read by moonlight, or perhaps at all.

I wondered again, *Why is Grant helping me? He knows why I want to reach her. Not just to reach her, not just to understand everything that's happened, but to get rid of him.*

Why should I trust Grant?

I was crying, and the sea spray on my face felt like the extra tears I would have shed if I could.

"I want to go now," I said, releasing his arm. "It's not

safe. It's illegal. I'm not ready." A wave splashed hard against the rock and I felt my feet slip on the algae-slick surface, but I didn't want to touch Grant again, not even for balance. The full impact of where I was hit me with the slam of the water.

"Oh, come on." He grabbed my hand, and his fingers dug into my flesh. "Not *safe*. It's *illegal*. You sound like Clark."

"Maybe I do sound like Clark," I said. "Maybe I want to sound like Clark. And get your hand the hell off me. He and I won't let you come back if you do this."

Grant's grip softened. "I'm sorry," he said. "I'm really sorry. I was trying to help. I . . ."

"Let's just go," I said.

WE SAT IN THE car for a few minutes. I was soaking wet, freezing, clutching the urn of ashes, staring straight ahead, waiting for Grant to start the engine, but I could see peripherally that he was looking at me. And that he was enveloped in a pulsing, dark, emergency red light that didn't come from any discernable outside source. I thought of all the times I'd seen this color around Grant before—a reflection in a puddle, a flash of light from an ambulance on my wall, his eyes in my mind. How had I ignored such distinct warnings?

He leaned over and spoke into my neck so I could feel his breath move strands of my hair against my skin. "I'm sorry," he said. "I didn't mean to upset you. I was just trying to help. I don't have much time."

"What do you mean?"

"I want you, before it's too late."

I touched the sea spray that had dried in the wind on my face like tears. "Are you kidding? We came here to . . ." I pressed the urn of ashes to my chest. The ring on my finger was pulsing with the same red that I'd seen coming off Grant.

Why hadn't I checked the ring when I was with him before? Did he have me that deeply under his spell?

"Please, Julie, please, I need you. Now. I only have until tomorrow night. That's when the accident was. Then I'll have to leave."

"What are you talking about? Take me home," I said.

Grant's upper lip lifted slightly, showing his teeth. I rarely saw his teeth, only Clark's. Clark, who was always smiling, or used to always smile. "Whatever," Grant said. "Whatever. I don't know why I bother."

"Take me home," I said again.

He started the car and threw it into DRIVE so abruptly that it lurched over the side of the curb separating the parking area from the highway. Eminem blasted on the stereo. "No Love." "You need me, too," Grant muttered, his jaw set. "Without me you'll never feel good about yourself."

He hung a U-turn across the road. The canyon seemed to be collapsing around us. My body was shaking with the cold of my wet clothes in the night air and the colder sensation of fear. The red light coming off Grant was even stronger now, like flames reflected in glass. I could see colors around people, my dreams were full of messages. Ed Rainwater had said I had a gift, some kind of spiritual ability that could be developed. I had a friend who cared about me, though I had pushed him away. I had a grandmother who had loved me.

"I don't need you anymore," I said to Grant.

He turned to look at me as the car sped even faster into the dark ahead. "It doesn't matter anyway, babe. I've got his body now, don't I? And if he doesn't get rid of me by tomorrow night"—he cocked his finger at me—"I'm here to stay forever."

Sick chills went through my body like the kind you get before you vomit, and my mouth tasted like iron.

"What?" I shouted over the sounds blaring inside my head and out. "I thought you said . . ."

"Never trust the dead. I said I have to leave by tomorrow, but it's only *if* you figure out how to get rid of me at the right time. Otherwise I get to stay, friend."

"He's stronger. He's going to come back."

"Not if I scare the shit out of him."

The car was speeding now, racing along the highway.

Grant turned off into Topanga.

"Where are you going?"

"Driving. I'm driving." He reached down between the seats and took out an open bottle of wine. Held it up. "Want some?"

"Put that away. What the hell are you doing?" I tried to grab it from him, but he moved his arm and some of the wine spattered red drops onto the seat. "What the fuck?" I said.

"This is how the driver was doing it. Just wanted to take his girlfriend out for a little spin, thought the wine would be romantic, didn't think he'd kill anybody! Anybody young and gifted with his whole fucking life ahead of him. Didn't think that! They never do, they never do. Ask MADD, Mothers Against Drunk—"

"Stop it, Grant, please." I tried to speak softly, reaching out and touching his arm.

The car took another curve, and I slammed against the side door. Here it was. I could die now. I could give up all the loneliness and stress and pain and loss that was life and just leave with him. But I didn't want to.

There were two boys. The brave one, the frightened one. The bold one, the timid. The tough one, the sweet one. The dead one and the one who was still alive, so far anyway, if his brother allowed it.

215

"Clark!"

"Stop it," Grant said. "Stop crying for him every time you're scared. He's gone. You're with me now. And the Clark man hates fast things." He winked at me. "Maybe that's why he likes you."

"He's not gone." I tried to focus on Clark, to use whatever gifts I might have to overcome Grant and bring Clark back to me.

I thought of the day in Chinatown with Clark, the straw hat he bought, the purple parasol, the way he had noticed everything—red paper lanterns, metal dragons inlaid in the pavement, sour plum candies. The trip to the Arboretum, chasing each other from the willow hut, the red-and-white Queen Anne, small in the distance like a playhouse, his laughter, his touch. Yes, if I tried hard enough, I could see him, I could feel him. It was as if he was here with me.

"Clark!" I shouted. "Clark, I need you. Come back!"

"How are you ever going to live like that?" A snicker. "He's more helpless than you are."

"You're never going to live," I said. "So stop, okay? Just stop." I was screaming as Grant sped around another curve. Along the side of the canyon the dark rocks fell into nothingness below.

I pressed the urn even closer to my heart. I squeezed my eyes shut, and this time I thought of her, my grandma, trying to conjure her up, if just for this moment. Her face was floating in front of me, and I could see her green eyes shining and shining with so much tenderness. I didn't want to go to her; I wanted to stay on this earth and carry her around in my heart where she already was.

"Clark," I said again, softer now.

The car lurched toward the side of the road, toward the abyss.

There was a screech of brakes and I slammed forward toward the dash as the car spun sideways and skidded, and I thought we were dying and there was something I wanted to tell Clark, something I wanted to say.

The car stopped.

I opened my eyes and looked at the boy next to me. A boy giving off the same glow of sun-through-leaf-green light that shone in my ring. He was panting and shaking. He reached across the seat and took my hand and held it flat against his chest where his heart was pounding, pounding, pounding.

It was Clark.

THE GOOD-BYE

He took my face in his hands, cheekbones cupped by fingers, and looked into my eyes. "You're okay, right? You're okay? I came back in time? I didn't let him hurt you?"

I fell against him, crying, and we sat in the car on the edge of that cliff, as the sun of the new year crested the rocky landscape with streaks of red and gold, my grandmother's urn beside us.

"What did he mean about tomorrow night?" I kept repeating the words, unable to stop.

"What are you talking about?" Clark asked, and I explained what Grant had said.

"It's the anniversary of his death," Clark said.

"He said we'd either have to make him leave or he'd take over your body," I told him.

Clark shook his head. "Like hell he will. You've got a learner's permit, right?" He got out of the car and went around to the trunk, and I followed him. He pulled a length of rope out of the back. His gaze and his hands were steady.

"What's this?" I asked him.

He sat in the passenger seat. "Tie my hands together, so I can't grab the wheel."

"No way, Clark. I'm not tying you up. I'm not into S and M," I tried to joke.

But his eyes weren't laughing and his face was so serious, he could have been Grant. He kept holding the rope out to me. "Do it, Julie," he said. He wasn't messing around.

At one point on the way home, I saw him flinch and writhe on the seat, mumbling to himself, and a red siren light flashed a warning in my brain, but he shut his eyes, put his hands on his knees, and began to take long, even breaths.

When we got to my apartment I untied him; he had rope burns on his wrists. I gave him a bottle of aloe, wanting to put it on him myself but afraid to touch him.

We took our herbal tinctures from Daiyu, applied our gem essences from Tatiana, and ate a porridge Clark had in his backpack made of millet, goji berries, raw honey, and ghee.

Both of us were exhausted, but we were afraid to sleep

so we made ourselves stay up listening to music all afternoon. Clark also made me tie his wrists again although I didn't want to.

At around 4:00 the phone rang—PRIVATE CALLER—and I answered it.

"Hi? Julie?"

"Yes?" I said. No one except Grant and Mrs. Carol ever called me, and I searched my brain for who this girl could be.

"It's Ally," she said.

"Oh, hi." And then I asked, "Are you okay?" Her voice sounded so soft and shaky.

Clark cocked his head at me and I gestured for him to wait. My pulse was accelerating and my head hurt.

"I wanted to thank you," Ally said. "For warning me? About Jason. He and his friends came over the other night. They wanted to come in. They were drunk and I was by myself and I told them no. I wouldn't have really thought about it except . . . you know, when you said that thing? So I put the alarm on and I called my parents. And those guys tried to break in. They were saying they were going to . . ." She stopped, and it sounded like she was crying.

"But you're okay?" I said.

"Yeah, I'm okay. My parents got home in time. But if you hadn't said that . . ."

"Thank you for telling me, Ally," I said. I looked over at

Clark and all I wanted was to rest my head against his chest and close my eyes.

IN THE EARLY EVENING, we both fell asleep—me on my bed, Clark in the armchair in my room—and woke at the same time a little before midnight. I checked to make sure it was Clark sitting there watching me in the darkened room, and not Grant.

I untied him, we lit candles and sage, sprayed the rose-water, and scattered mugwort everywhere. We sat facing each other and held hands. I did Amrita's breath work and it felt easier this time. No thoughts or visions interfered. Counting the breaths, thinking only of the breath. I imagined my cells rapidly vibrating, imagined the room flooding with rose-quartz-colored light. Then Clark and I put our fingers on the marker.

"Grandma," I said. "Please come now."

A stillness in the room, an intake of breath, a warmth in my throat and chest. *I love you,* I thought.

And then, just then, the marker gently arced to YES. Simple as that. But not simple at all. It had taken us so much work just to be able to receive this one single, precious word.

"Is this you?"

YES.

I blinked away the instant tears that seemed to have

come back with me from the Pacific. Finding her this way was harder than I had thought. It made her feel both closer and more distant. There were so many things I wanted to share with her. But I had to stay focused on the task at hand.

"Is there something you can tell us?"

Clark and I sat upright and still, staring at the board. The marker stayed still, too, for what felt like a long time. Then, slowly, slowly, it began to move.

The little plastic marker, the child's toy, spelled out a simple and overused word, one that everyone knows and says all the time, one that we have forgotten to believe in as the magic that it is. It stood for what I felt for my grandmother and what she felt for me. It stood for what I felt for Clark and for what, by letting him go, Clark and I could now feel for his dead and despairing twin.

Clark looked deep into my eyes, candlelight flaring in his dark irises. His face was solemn but calm. "What are we going to do?" he asked me.

I could see my grandmother's face, the way I saw it floating in front of me in the car. I had spent so much time looking for her that I hadn't realized that she was with me all the time. In the dress at Treasure Hunt, the paper with the information about Ed Rainwater, the vision with the singing women, the roses that practically fell into my hands, the rainbow in the desert, the arrival of my best friend.

Clark and I had gone seeking guidance and I had been told I had a gift inherited from my father, but maybe my grandmother was the real guide, the real shaman; maybe a shaman is just someone who understands that life is filled with loss and pain and that love, that simple, overused word, is really the most important thing, the only thing we have to fight with, the thing that always, ultimately wins.

I knew what to do.

"Do you have a picture of him?" I asked.

Clark took out his wallet and opened it. Tucked in the back was a small snapshot of a boy who looked a lot like him but with a more muscular build, a more erect posture, innate confidence creating angles in his face that his twin didn't have. Looking at the image, I saw that Grant was not really a voracious ghost, not a demonic spirit; he wasn't just emptiness and devastation. He was only a beautiful boy who had died too soon leaving emptiness and devastation in his wake. Leaving things that needed to be slowly, slowly healed.

And something else was different, besides the way I saw Grant.

Clark and I, we were different. Clark had almost lost me and himself and was no longer afraid to let Grant go, and I no longer needed Grant because I had Clark—Clark who now had internalized his brother's strength, without his despair and hunger. Clark, who was my best friend, even though I hadn't always treated him that way. Clark, the one I loved. He was deep inside my heart. And so was my grandma.

"Please release us from all the grief and fear that holds us back," I said. "Please release the spirit who clings to us. We no longer need him and he no longer needs us. We are ready to let him go. Please let him go back to his dimension without harming anyone, without devastation or emptiness. Knowing he was loved and is still loved."

The candle flame leaped and spat, and the sage smoked so that the air billowed with it. My lungs burned as I inhaled sharply. I looked at my hand. It trembled and the ring was flickering back and forth. Green. Red. Green. Red. I looked up and saw the boy sitting in front of me. Not my best friend. The other boy. The boy in the photo. I forced myself to speak calmly, as if I wasn't ready to run screaming from the room.

"Good-bye, Grant," I said to him, soft but firm, the way you speak to a child you must leave. "We love you but it's time."

He reached out his hand as if he was trying to touch me, but I wouldn't let him. I told myself not to look away: *Breathe, Julie. Keep breathing.*

"Clark," I said.

He lowered his gaze.

"I'm sorry I hurt you, Clark," I said. I'm so sorry."

When he looked back up at me, my ring was green and so was the light around my best friend.

He reached out and took my hand, folding my fingers up in his. This time he was Clark and I let him. I knew he had made his final choice to stay.

"Good-bye, Grant." There were tears thickening Clark's voice, but his face was calm. "I'm sorry, brother. I won't forget you."

It was 12:04. The room was suddenly quiet and I realized the refrigerator had been banging incessantly and now was not. The putrid smell evaporated, replaced by an intense aroma of roses mixed with the medicinal smoke of sage. I collapsed onto the floor. Clark put his arms around me. I could feel his heart beating hard through his shirt, the way you might feel your twin's heart, if you were a twin being born.

WE FELL ASLEEP LIKE this and later that night I dreamed about the red tattoo on my arm again. This time the letters, the very same letters, spelled something different in reverse.

Not *E-V-I-L*.

L-I-V-E

THE NEXT DAY, I woke my mother from an afternoon nap in her room.

"I need to talk to you." She blinked at me as if she didn't recognize me for a second, and I practiced my breath. Even. In and out. "I need to tell you some things."

"Okay." She moved over so I could sit beside her on the bed. It smelled only of the pear-and-citrus soap she used.

"I've been having the dreams again. Like when I was a kid."

"What type of dreams?"

"Nightmares. Weird things. Since Grandma died."

"Why didn't you tell me?"

Instead of answering I went on. "I saw these colors around her, right before she died, and sometimes I see them around you and Clark. Around Luke before the accident. And I hear music. Or loud sounds."

"What do you mean? You see colors around people? And you hear sounds that aren't there?"

I nodded.

My mother hugged me so quickly, I didn't have time to pull away and I was secretly glad of that. "Why didn't you tell me, Julie?"

I just looked at her, literally holding my tongue between my teeth, trying not to say something harsh.

"I've been so absent," she said. "I know. I'm so sorry. We have to take you to a doctor. A psychiatrist."

"I will if you want, but I'm not worried about it. That's

not why I told you. I think I know how to handle it. I just wanted to let you know."

I avoided mentioning Grant, but I explained to my mom about Daiyu and Tatiana, Ed and Amrita.

At this she stopped me. "He lives in Joshua Tree? And he's Cherokee?"

"Yes," I said, a cool prickling in my spine.

"And how did you find him?"

I told her about the advertisement in my grandmother's poetry book.

She shook her head. "I knew she was up to something," she said.

I asked her what she meant. *Breathe. In and out. Breathe.*

"Your grandmother started researching who your father was. I told her I didn't want her to do it, it wasn't even ethical, but she said she thought it was important for you to know. Especially when you started having the nightmares. I'm not sure, but I think this man might be him."

"Ed Rainwater." Tall, Native American, a degree in psychology. He had said, *I had a practice there, but I can help people better when I'm not constantly fighting my environment.* I could see Amrita looking at me in a way I didn't understand when I had told her about my sperm-donor father.

A rose-colored wave of warmth rushed through my body, obliterating any chill, gathering all the broken pieces of me in its wake and joining them together into a cohesive whole. I could see my grandmother's face, the smile she had given me before she died. Maybe she was going to tell me about my father. But there was something even more important she was going to say. I knew the words; she had said them to me a million times before. The three most important words in the world. And I knew it was her love that had led me to Clark and to my father, away from Grant, and then, finally, back to myself.

EPILOGUE

For the senior prom that spring I wore a vintage dress from Treasure Hunt. Mrs. Carol had insisted I accept it as a present when she found out who my prom date was. ("See, I told you he was special," she'd scolded me.) The dress was made of cream and pink lace. I removed the sleeves and made it strapless, kept it long, almost to the ground, and wore it under a short pink faux fur jacket my mom had bought me with the money from her first paycheck at her new writing job. She promised she would start saving for a house again, right away, and not buy any more fake furs after this one. At first it had seemed too frivolous to wear, but it looked cute with the dress and my long, pink false eyelashes, my hair in a loose updo.

When I reached inside my grandma's black needlepoint

purse with the wreaths of pink roses, I found an old lipstick that had belonged to her. Somehow I hadn't discovered it before. It was cherry red in a gold dispenser and smelled like powder and wax.

Beside it, in the purse, was a small sprig of sage from Ed Rainwater. I hadn't contacted him since my mom told me that she thought he was my father. Someday, though, I knew I would go back there and speak to him.

Clark arrived in his parents' car. He had rented a tuxedo with tails and wore the top hat Grant had on at Ally Kellogg's party. I kissed his cheek and he blushed, but instead of looking away he stared right into my eyes and hugged me so that I could feel the reassuring beat of his heart. He had a corsage of tea roses for me to wear. Pink, apricot, and gold roses like our magic ones.

My mom took our picture, hugged Clark, winked at me. She was very into the idea of him as my boyfriend but, of course, she didn't know our whole story. It might be different then. (*Yeah, Mom, there was a dead version, too.*)

"Don't stay out too late," she said, but she didn't sound forlorn, even though she'd be alone, without Luke or any other creepy man. She had been enjoying her solo nights of takeout and Netflix, she said. Clark and I had promised her we'd join her on Sunday evening.

As we left I looked back at her standing in the window.

Maybe it was from the rose-colored bulbs she'd put in the lamps in the house, but she glowed with a clear pink light.

Instead of going straight to the prom, we stopped at the house, my house, as I still thought of it in the secret world inside me. I stood on the lawn, looking at the FOR SALE/FORE-CLOSURE sign, the empty windows, the trees dressed softly by the couturier of spring.

I will come back here someday, I said to the fig and the avocado and the jacaranda, the banana and the birds-of-paradise, the grapes growing over the arbor, the mermaid-tiled pool. *I'll learn about psychology, but also meditation and herbs, all the ways to help people and I'll come back and live here. I'll buy you back. Someday. I promise, Grandma.*

Then I turned and ran with Clark down among the cypresses back to his car.

WE DROVE UP TO the flamingo-pink, terracotta-roofed Beverly Hills Hotel, along the wide drive lined with palm trees. Clark held my arm as we walked to the entrance. People looked at us, pretending they weren't. Ally Kellogg gave me a baby-powder-and-jasmine-scented hug and complimented my dress. I knew Clark and I looked good, working our nerdy, matching glasses. I felt bigger and warmer and for a moment didn't know how to identify the feeling. Until I realized: I was happy.

They took our photograph at the entrance, Clark's whole body draped around me like a shawl, heating me through my lace dress.

There was some dancing going on in the chandelier-lit ballroom with the skirted tables. I'd never seen Clark dance. He pulled me out onto the floor in spite of the crappy music, waving his arms around, surprisingly graceful, after all, despite his gangly limbs.

"I didn't know you danced," I said.

"Yeah. About as good as I play basketball. But you know, you only live once, or most of us do, so I said to myself, I said, 'Clark, man, just go for it.'"

We laughed and danced and danced. We ate the lousy food.

"I wish I brought some *kicharee*," Clark said.

"Don't tease me." I put down my fork. Chicken in cream sauce, iceberg lettuce salad, and a few dwarfish vegetables just couldn't compare.

To add insult to injury "Call Me Maybe" was playing for the second time that night. "They should have had you cater and DJ," I said.

He speared a tiny piece of canned baby corn and tilted it back and forth, making it dance to the song. "Is this an actual vegetable or are they manufactured from plastic for important engagements such as this one?"

We laughed so hard, the snaps on the side of my dress popped, and then he tried to fasten them for me, his fingers too big for the task, and we laughed some more.

I wanted to laugh like that—doubled over, spasming for the rest of my life. Clark made me laugh like that. Sometimes you just want someone who can make you forget the person you wished you had never become, and make you remember who you were before.

"I'm going to miss you," Clark said suddenly. He had stopped laughing and I did, too, then. The chandelier lights were reflecting in his glasses.

"I'll miss you too."

He'd gotten into MIT, and I had a scholarship to Stanford. We had both been so excited by our acceptance letters that we hadn't paid much attention to how far away the two schools were, and though I'd thought about it since then, we hadn't discussed it.

"I'll visit you," he said. "I mean, if that's okay?"

"Of course! You better." I grabbed his hand. "Hey, I actually like this song! Finally."

We danced some more to Lady Gaga, "Born This Way." Then he took my arm and danced me out through the doors into the garden.

There was a little stream, the banks covered with moss and flowers. I couldn't see them, but I smelled and felt them in the darkness. Gardenias and impatiens. Clark took off his glasses, pocketed them, and then, very gently, took off mine.

"Remember what the Ouija board said that night?" he asked me.

I did.

"It's a very good word," Clark said.

"Yes it is. A very good word."

And so, there in the garden, Clark and I used that very, very good word.

I leaned in to kiss him with lips painted with Grandma Miriam's lipstick. I didn't levitate or fly into space. I was on earth in a sparkling garden kissing my beloved best, best friend and that is where I wanted to stay.

As I opened my eyes, I saw there were reflections in his, like light on the stream water. Just as I had imagined him that morning, when I sat at my altar in front of my white candle for healing, my green one for luck, and my red one for knowledge (for danger can bring knowledge, my departed ghost), the picture of my grandmother, the picture of Grant, and a picture of my mother, me, and Clark, learning how to breathe.